The Case of the Mountain's Monster

Rhiannon D. Elton

The Case of the Mountain's Monster © Rhiannon D. Elton 2022
The Wolflock Cases: Book 10
Second edition

ISBN: 978-0-6487636-9-7 (paperback)

First Edition published March 2022

info@rhiannoneltonauthor.com

Cover compiled by Rhiannon D. Elton

This is a work of fiction. Names, characters, places, and incidents either are the products of the author's imagination or are used fictitiously. Any resemblance to actual persons, living or dead, businesses, companies, events, or locales is entirely coincidental.

Cataloguing-in-Publication information for this title is listed with the National Library of Australia.

Published in Australia by Rhiannon D. Elton and Pelaia Adventures

This project is supported by the Regional Arts Development Fund (RADF). RADF is a partnership between the Queensland Government and Logan City Council to support arts and culture in regional Queensland.

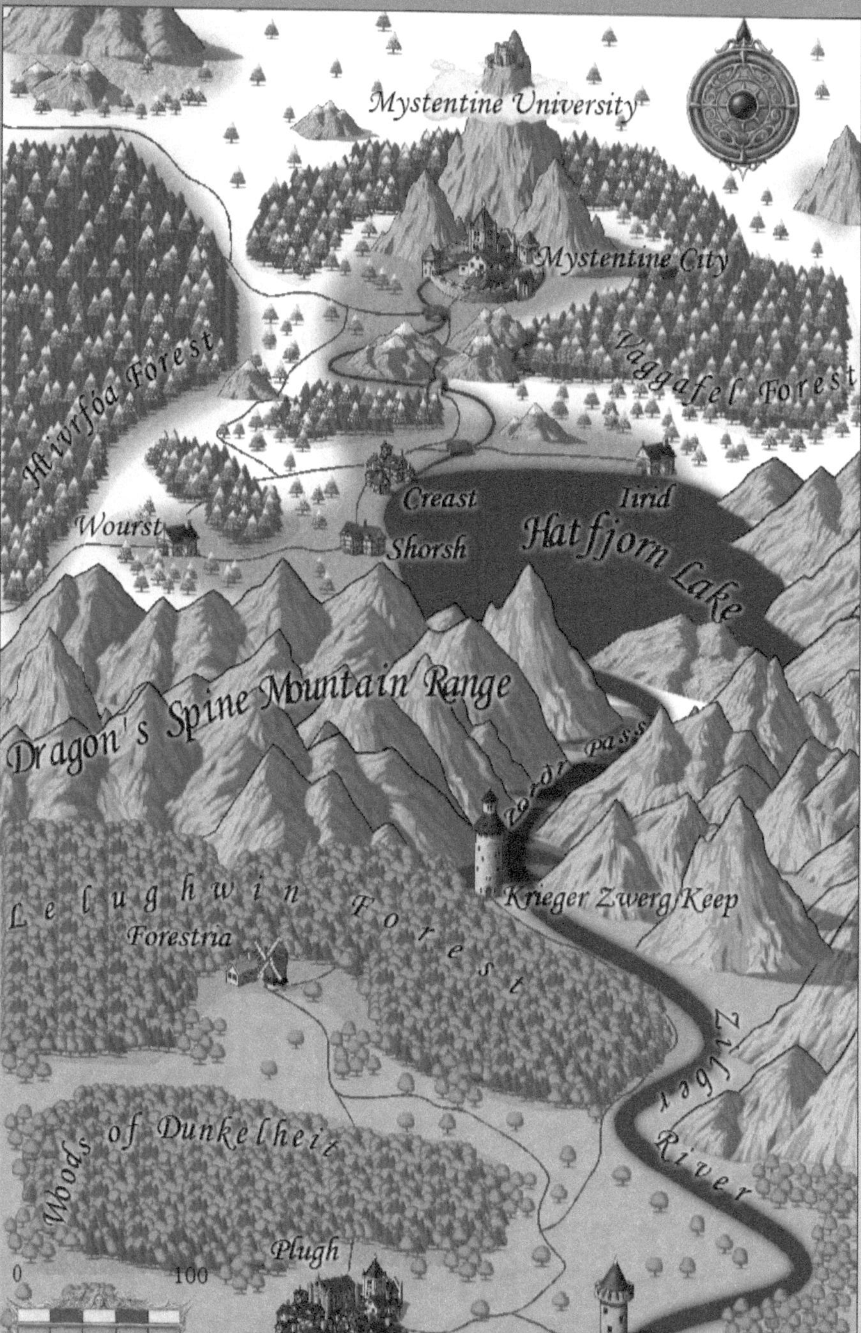
Mystentine University
Mystentine City
Vaggafel Forest
Htivrfóa Forest
Creast
Iirid
Wourst
Shorsh
Hatfjorn Lake
Dragon's Spine Mountain Range
pass
Krieger Zwerg Keep
Lelughwin Forest
Forestria
River
Woods of Dunkelheit
Plugh
0
100
Scale in Miles
Seebruecke Dock
Woods of Veil
(c) 2018 Rhiannon D. Elton

Declaration of Intention

Merry meet,

The purpose of the books the author writes is to give representation to as many peoples, creatures and landscapes as they can. Although written from the perspective of a Caucasian teenage boy, the author hopes to offer a light into the harmony of different cultures and creeds of people. The author's aim is to promote harmony, understanding and compassion in all areas, while also inspiring readers to stand up against injustice and be critical thinkers in life.

While the author does their best to research, interview and highlight the best parts of people, they are only human and can make mistakes. The author asks you gently educate them by sending them an email in order to discuss anything that may have caused harm to a group of people unintentionally.

The author believes that the cure for ignorance is education, but please approach the topic cordially in order to avoid any knee-jerk cognitive dissonance.

Finally, the viewpoints displayed in the books comes from a particular character and is not necessarily that of the author's. The author seeks to display flaws, growth and human nature on many levels, and hopes that you will analyse the character of the protagonist without adopting any negative behaviours from them.

Merry part, and merry meet again.

Get More of the Magic & Mystery...

subscribe.rhiannoneltonauthor.com/more

If you want more clues, more magic and more mystery, let me know by going to the Wolflock Cases subscribe page.

You'll get clues, maps, sketches, behind the scenes stories, lore and much more! You'll also be the first to know when a new story is coming out so you can solve the mystery before your friends.

If you sign up with the magical link below, you'll also get a free downloadable map to follow Wolflock's journey to Mystentine University.

subscribe.rhiannoneltonauthor.com/more

Dedicated to all of my Patrons,

With your belief in me I have all the magic I need. You are as much part of the stories as the ink on the page.

Kristel Anderson, Fellow Ciga'm Librarian
Cassie Davis, Queen of Badassery
Carolyn Ferrando, Siren of Socials
Lisa King, Priestess of Ancient Libraries
Carly Reading, Archmage of Getting Things Done
Karen Sullivan, Mother Fae and Goblin (me)
Nikki Verral, Elven Princess

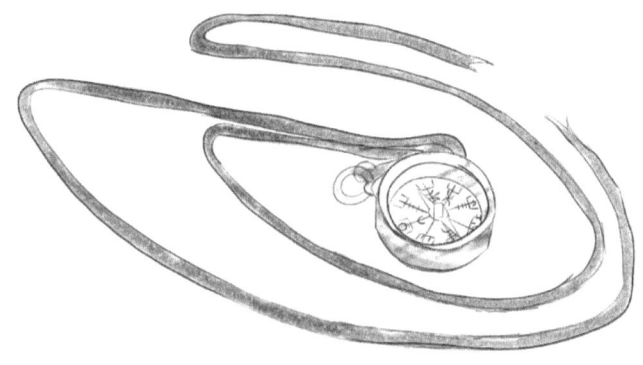

CHAPTER 1

The First of the Last Steps

"Mr Wolflock Felen?"

"Present!"

His hand trembled in the air with electric excitement as he looked up at the mountain. He brought it back down and gripped his satchel strap as if it were the only thing holding him to the ground.

Wolflock felt as if he were looking at this moment as if it were his favourite painting. To his right stood the mountain he was set to climb to reach his final destination. To his left, his sombre best friend, staring at the guide as he rattled off the names of the people joining their trip.

"Ms Pakuna Cheyenne?"

"Y-yes!" gulped a lean woman with the same reddish complexion and thick black hair as Tanni and Tinni. As Wolflock turned and caught her dark eyes, he wondered if she was a student or professor. She looked nervous with her thick hide shoes pointing into each other, but her stacks of paper suggested she already had research planned. Fresh-faced, with research ready to go, told him she was a professor.

Unlike the young woman standing beside her with dark brown hair cut into a perfect bob. Although she also had stacks of papers, she brimmed with the confidence of someone who had made this trip a few times. Wolflock saw her gravitate towards some of the other students with familiarity, telling him she was a returning student.

"Fuddugol Calon?"

"Call me Fiddi," she called out as she closed her case of papers and passed it to the assistant loading the luggage onto the large wagon.

With a grin stretching from ear to ear, Wolflock's piercing blue eyes swept the group. Lija pleaded with her mother to join the hike from the veranda, but her mother clutched at her, afraid to be apart from her for a moment. Dr Växtadlare smiled at them both from the railing and Wolflock could see he was waiting for his moment to resolve their conflict without seeming too excited to provide the solution. His relaxed shoulders, but fidgety fingers and keen golden eyes gave him away.

The mountain guide's gravelly voice barked names over the chattering group, and had to repeat himself several times as the distracted company missed their roll call. The assistant guide took the details of the luggage and goods being taken up to the university. Wolflock saw her blonde eyebrows pinched as she argued with two men trying to load on three boxes that weren't on her list.

"Mothy," Wolflock nudged his friend in the arm and nodded to the wagon. "Do you think they're trying to get something to the university they don't want to declare? Or do you think they're just dull?"

His friend didn't respond and continued to stare forward at the mountain guide calling names.

"Professor Thuthukta Isisodwa?"

"Yes."

Wolflock turned at the alarmingly deep voice to see a man the size of Grogen with midnight dark skin and a thick scar closing his left eye. His one brown eye didn't look at the young boy, but Wolflock felt him scrutinising everyone in his peripheries. He wore practical hiking clothes, thick boots and a long, thin wooden pouch made of dark bamboo, but with no other defining features.

"What do you think he teaches? He's definitely not a student." He nudged Mothy again.

The blond boy reshuffled his bag as if it irritated him. He grunted a noncommittal reply and didn't break his line of sight from the guide.

"Tareq Shanif?"

"Are you feeling well?" Wolflock frowned.

Mothy's brown eyes stared forward. "I'm waiting for my name."

"Ah. Of course," Wolflock chuckled. He thought Mothy must be one of those people who has to anxiously wait for their name to be called so they can affirm their presence without embarrassment.

"Tareq Shanif?" the guide called again.

"Oh! Sorry. Yes. That's me," laughed a boy with a small gold trimmed turban who was not much older than Wolflock and Mothy, before returning to his conversation with another pair of students.

"Shǐmìsī Qiānqiān?"

Wolflock looked around to see if anyone with such a Xiayahn sounding name was not paying attention.

"Shǐmìsī Qiānqiān?" the guide called again,

louder.

The talk in the company seemed to grow as if it were trying to combat the roll call.

"Is Shǐmìsī Qiānqiān here?"

"They're not here, man, move on," called a boy the same age as Wolflock with a snide drawl.

A small wagon clattered on the road, pulling to a sharp halt at the end of the path. A girl with black hair pulled into a thick bun leaped from the front and scooped up bags of spices and herbs with her chubby arms.

"Thank you, Henrir!" She nodded a quick bow and ran down the path on her tippy toes. "I'm here! I'm here! Sorry I'm late!"

Wolflock had never seen a person with such dainty hands and feet with such a rotund waist. She looked like a curved spinning top.

"Shǐmìsī Qiānqiān?" the guide master repeated with a sigh.

"That's me. I'm so sorry I'm late. I was waiting on an order of saffron and dates, and they were very late. I'm so sorry."

Wolflock smiled at the newcomer, happy that they may have tasty food on the journey. He noticed her large bag had an odd rectangular shape to it, as if she filled it with containers for food. He also saw a chef's apron hooked through the top of her bag for easy access.

Miss Qiānqiān and Mothy are going to get along very well, he thought.

"Mr Mothy Enitnelav?"

Mothy drew in a breath and nodded. "That's me."

The two men trying to load on a large blanket chest were told off by the assistant as Shǐmìsī started loading her own items on before someone could log them. Wolflock and Mothy's belongings were some of the first loaded on, as well as a special tin of wild lettuce tea Wolflock had specifically requested.

"Mr Amery Blayne?"

"Feel better now?" Wolflock smirked. Mothy's face remained stony.

"I'm going to see if I can help," he mumbled, looking around everywhere except Wolflock's face.

"I'm sure they're fine. The Guard have paid for our journey, remember? You don't need to ingratiate yourself if you want to keep looking for details in our company with me."

"I want to."

"Very well. Who are we helping?" Wolflock looked around to see what was more interesting.

"No. That's fine. You keep people watching." The

frostiness in Mothy's tone stung, but Wolflock couldn't tell why.

"Mr Amery Blayne?"

As Mothy stepped away, the dark-haired boy frowned. Something was amiss. Was Mothy upset over something? He had mentioned nothing. Perhaps it was just nerves.

"Uh... very well. I'll... uh... see you when we get going."

Wolflock deflated as he stood alone in the crowd until he felt a heavy tug at his arm. Lija had grabbed him with her purplish white hands and swung her feet off the ground.

"Ma is going to let me go with you all to the first stop!" she giggled.

"Fantastic," he said, trying to keep the awkward tone out of his voice. "I'm not sure there will be much time to solve any problems along the way, though."

"Oh, that's fine. I get to show you the best way to travel up the mountain. There are lots of signs to watch out for. I can show you how to find fox dens, rabbit burrows, pine sap for cuts and grazes, and how to make places to keep warm. The tents can still get quite cold. And you have to set up four fingers from the sunset."

"Mr Amery Blayne? Are you here?"

As she chattered, Wolflock looked up at Ms Vuori and Dr Växtadlare for an explanation.

"If you hold your hand up so your fingers sit on the horizon, you generally have one hour until sunset," Ms Vuori said, reading his look and giving him the explanation.

"You're both joining us, then?" he asked, giving Lija one more swing before shaking his arm to get her to loosen her grip.

"Yes. I won't let her go anywhere without me, now. And this is the last trek for the year, so I thought it would be nice to see you all through to the first stop."

"And I don't get to make the journey often, so I thought the walk in the fresh air would do me good," Dr Växtadlare smiled, unable to keep his eyes off Ms Vuori.

"So, the guides haven't introduced themselves yet. What should I know about them?" Wolflock asked as the main blond guide called out for Amery Blayne again.

Ms Vuori looked fondly at her employees. "Well, Sangur is the lead guide. He's been with us for seven years now. He used to be a miner until an accident made him change careers. Now, he loves a good walk up and down the mountain. Best guide I have and a talented musician too. Ask him to play his guitar and you will have a great evening."

Wolflock nodded as he listened. He thought the chief guide looked too skinny to be a native of Shiriling, but, then, to hear that he'd gone from mining to walking for a living, it made sense that he had slimmed down.

"Urgi is our new recruit. She's as hard as nails and a stickler for details. It's a much easier trip when there are two to help. You'd be amazed at how many people don't know how to put up a basic tent."

Wolflock laughed, but looked away. He'd never slept in a tent in his life, let alone put one up.

"Mr Amery Blayne? Last call." Sangur shouted over the group, blowing his long moustache and beard as he spoke.

"Yes, yes. I'm here," drawled the blond boy, irritated he had to break off his conversation with the other students to respond. Wolflock raised a dark eyebrow at the insolence of the boy. "You don't have to yell."

Sangur's face reddened, but Ms Vuori stepped up next to him and let him know three more would accompany them.

"Urgi. Get the goats," he shouted when Ms Vuori finished.

"Yes sir. Do you have extra cargo on your forms, sir?" Urgi asked as the delivery men loaded on two more crates.

"Extra cargo? I'll look while you get the goats. Hitch 'em and we'll get going."

Wolflock didn't know how goats were going to pull the heavily laden cart up the mountain. Not only were there six tent bundles, as well as every person's non-essential luggage and post to Mystentine University, but the extra supplies built up the mound of packages high above the wagon.

"Merry meet, intrepid travellers." Sangur tapped the name sheet and took out a bag. Wolflock looked about and saw Mothy standing by the back of the wagon, checking the ropes holding everything down. The boy named Amery Blayne continued to talk, even though the other two students stood at attention. "I'm going to call your names a final time and then you can begin walking up the mountain path. We're going to stop for lunch at the fae portal, Aevingratt. You can't miss it. You also can't get lost if you stick to the road. After that, we will continue on as a group with me at the front and Urgi at the back with the wagon. I hope your legs are strong because the last day of our journey is going to be through a foot of snow if we're unlucky."

"Let's hope we're lucky," Wolflock grinned, but no one around him responded.

"We have a few rules to go over. You, Amery. What did I just say?" The blond boy froze at the sound of his name and finally stopped talking. "That's what I thought. Now listen up, and listen good. These rules are going to save your life if you follow them."

Urgi returned with two of the largest goats Wolflock had seen in his entire life; giant dark brown shaggy things with sagging skin folds and horns that twisted up into the shape of a lyre behind their heads. They moved like docile rolling boulders into position and allowed Urgi to harness them in, receiving the occasional carrot to snack on.

"Thanks," one of them rumbled as it chewed the vegetable in its slack jaw.

"Good manners, Dergi." Urgi wobbled the giant goat's neck folds and began mouthing Sangur's speech.

"Rule number one: never leave the group. If you wander off in this mountain you can get lost. If you get lost, it means you will be without shelter and friends. If you are without shelter and friends, you will most definitely freeze. If you freeze, we can only dig you out after you thaw in the Spring."

Wolflock looked around the company for their reactions. Mothy and the large professor, Thuthukta, remained stony faced. Ms Pakuna, Shĭmìsī, Blayne and the young girl he had spoken to looked anxious. The older boy and Fiddi rolled their eyes, having heard this warning speech before.

"Rule number two, never lose sight of the road. If nature calls, you'll have to go behind a tree. There aren't any portable bathrooms along the way, but whatever you do, keep sight of the road. If you lose sight of the road, you will lose the group. If you lose the group, you will get lost. If you get lost, it means you will be without shelter and friends. If you are without shelter and friends, you will most definitely freeze. If you freeze, we can only dig you out after you thaw in the Spring."

Wolflock sensed a trend.

"Rule number three, your gear is your life. Look after it. Put up your tent as per the instructions, keep your shoes on the road. Stay dry. If you don't look after your gear, you will freeze. If you freeze..."

Wolflock copied Urgi as he mouthed the second part of the rule.

"Rule number four, respect the weather. Stay with the group because Urgi and I are the only ones who know how to read the weather and keep you all safe. If you don't respect the weather, you will freeze. If you freeze..."

Wolflock memorised the rules more out of amusement than believing they were serious tools.

Never leave the group.
Never lose sight of the road.
Your gear is your life. Look after it.
Respect the weather
Shelter, Water, Food. In that order.
Don't tread on powder snow. (You don't know
what's under it)
Move at light, stay warm at night.

"And finally," Sangur gave a grin to Urgi, "don't stare into the darkness. It just might stare back."

Wolflock rolled his eyes. He'd already been through some of the most frightening times of his life. A creepy anecdote meant to keep the company behaving would not scare him.

"Now, as I call you, come and collect your compasses. Keep them on you at all times. They'll keep you from getting lost and they're enchanted to keep away bad weather. Etienne and Drua Merris," Sangur waved at the pair Blayne had been speaking to.

Wolflock could tell they were brother and sister because of the same shade of golden red hair and honey brown eyes. They also both sported faces filled with freckles and were rugged up from head to toe as if they were in the pits of Winter, rather than the end of Autumn.

"We'll get a head start. I'm sure Heilari would like to collect ingredients along the way." Ms Vuori patted Wolflock's shoulder as they walked ahead, the two adults swinging Lija's arms back and forth.

Besides the Vuori's and Dr Växtadlare, the company going to the top of the mountain numbered twelve. Mothy was called up next and received his necklace, walking up the path with the Merris siblings. Why didn't he look back? Was he not going to wait? What was so interesting about this pair?

Professor Thuthukta went next, hand on the cap of his bamboo cylinder, then Tareq with his gold trimmed turban, Shǐmìsī collected hers and waited for Ms Pakuna to meet her at the treeline.

"Mr Felen. Up you come." Sangur waved him up. Blue tattoos covered his hand in knotted sigils and bands. Wolflock jogged forward, hoping to catch up with Mothy. "Now, do not take this off. It might very well save your life."

"Uh... I'm sure it will." Wolflock took the necklace and put it on, feeling like he was being given a medal without knowing the true significance of it. Without another word, he strode along the path with one last look back at the city. The elevation allowed him to see the two walls hugging the city and part of the road leading away to Creast. He'd journeyed so far. These final steps brought him the closest he'd ever been to his destination. As long as he made it to the university, he'd never have to take a step backwards. He'd never have to return to Plugh against his wishes.

The birds in the trees chirped at him as they protected their stores for Winter. The wind blew past him as if it had somewhere urgent to be. Unlike their haunted journey from Creast to Mystentine, being able to see the city through the trees and smell the wood smoke from chimneys made him feel as if he could keep his bearings easily. Maybe it was the compass.

Wolflock turned the brass instrument over in his hands. The disc wobbling in the middle of the device sat behind glass, but, unlike the compass on the Silver Ice Hair, wasn't in water.

That makes sense. In these temperatures, the water might freeze, Wolflock thought to himself. On the back was a sigil he imagined was an ancient symbol to promote good weather. It didn't look active, but it was antique. The compass dial differed from any he'd seen before. Unlike the Southern ones with clear North, South, East and West inscriptions, this one sported eight tridents in various shapes. The Northern pointing one comprised three prongs and three lines cutting the stem. As he walked, he made a quick sketch of it so he could see if it had magical properties when he reached the university.

"Felen!"

Wolflock recognised the voice of the rude blond boy from earlier and ignored him as he finished his sketch.

"Felen, hold up a moment, will you?"

Wolflock didn't change his pace.

"Pah," panted the boy as he arrived in step. "Well now, what a terribly droll speech. Freeze to death in nine different ways. Hah."

Wolflock snapped his journal closed and put it in his pocket before looking at the boy properly.

"Huh. Same vest. Of course, mine isn't as old as yours." The boy smiled, but it didn't reach his eyes.

"I beg your pardon, but this came from... oh." Wolflock realised they were wearing the same vest and jacket set, but the blond boy wore one made of paisley baby blue embroidered thread on cream cotton. "You're from Grothener too."

It irritated Wolflock that this rude boy shared anything with him, let alone a tailor.

"That's right! How observant you are, Felen. Amery Blayne from Pemshire. Capital of the Fferm province. You're going to study at the university, too, are you not?"

"How very astute of you, Blayne. I take it," Wolflock looked him up and down, "you're going to study the political sciences?"

"Oh, goodness no. You sound like my mother," Blayne laughed. "No, no, no. I'm going into the literary arts. None of that hard work stuff. No. My mental prowess is far more aligned with the poetic and romantic."

Gross. Wolflock made a face. "I'm sure it is."

"And you?" Blayne asked, rolling his shoulders as he walked.

"I'm not sure yet. I'll consult the guidance counsellors when I arrive."

"Ah. One of those ones, eh?" Blayne chuckled and nudged Wolflock with his pointy elbow.

"What do you mean?" Wolflock eyed him in the corner of his vision.

"Oh, you know," Blayne chuckled. "The lost and the wandering. Disillusioned with home or without any prospects. You got all dressed up in your Relimpus best to make a good impression, but for who and for what?"

Blayne sighed his string of words as if it were some tragic play. He reminded Wolflock of Veluse from the Silver Ice Hair, but with less charm.

"You're very presumptuous. Firstly, my friend and I have been travelling for months and interacting with the local environments." He thought about crawling through tight spaces and crates on the Silver Ice Hair, dancing, working on the ship, racing through Creast to clean the bay, and solving mysteries in the forests South of Mystentine. "And secondly-"

"Oh! That's your friend? I thought he was your servant. Hah! What strange company you keep, Felen. Strange indeed."

Wolflock's mouth pulled to the side, and his nose twitched. "Mothy is more competent than anyone I know. He's studying to be one of the most accomplished doctors I've ever seen. He's a practical man. These are the best travelling clothes for our journey."

"I suppose that explains the state of your outfit, then. Not as good at planning travels as your friend? I'm sure your friend is learning a lot from Merris. He's already the best student doctor in Mystentine."

Wolflock said nothing. The more Amery Blayne spoke, the less Wolflock liked him. And he'd started in a low position of likeableness.

Blayne soon complained about having to walk and how they didn't provide shoes suitable for the journey. He boasted about his mother's social standing and how his father was some kind of successful envoy for Fferm.

Wolflock had never been more relieved to see the Antrum mother and daughter.

"Mr Wolflock!" Lija waved. "Come pick a good stick with us."

Ms Vuori smiled with her arms filled with sticks and branches.

"Is the doctor breaking rule number two?" Wolflock asked, taking the branch Lija passed for him to try out.

"No, no," Dr Växtadlare chuckled as he returned, dropping a handful of flowers into his pouch. "Just foraging. I definitely need to come up here more. This is lovely."

Wolflock couldn't help but see how the doctor smiled at Ms Vuori as he spoke.

"Shall we catch up to the others?" Wolflock swapped his branch with another, straighter, one, which Lija took and tested on the ground before giving it back, satisfied.

He felt grateful that Ms Vuori and Dr Växtadlare would become Blayne's new people to brag to, but to his dismay, the pompous boy maintained his belligerent focus on him all the way to where the others had slowed and congregated. He smiled and took steps towards Mothy, who was in a smiling, animated conversation with the Merris siblings, when something caught his arm.

"Wolflock! Show me how this stick could be used in the theft of a priceless artefact while also being the key tool for rescuing orphans from a burning barn." Lija swung on the sticks with gusto.

Wolflock opened his mouth, then laughed. "That is a fanciful conundrum. Let's see. Judging by the knots on the stick, it is of a very sturdy quality, and, thankfully, it is still green, meaning it won't catch on fire in that burning barn of yours."

He proceeded to entertain the child and her family with intricate details of the trophies she picked up and how they could be used in her elaborate scenarios until they reached the glade with the fae portal.

Two trees made of crystal clear ice grew out of the frosty clearing and reached to one another, forming an arch. Looking through the archway at different angles showed different scenes of a beautiful Winter garden.

"Is there someone in there?" gasped the Merris sister. "I just saw someone in there!"

"Don't be foolish, Drua," her brother scoffed. "As

I was saying, Mr Enitnelav, the trick with all aches and pains is to apply the coldest of ice. By sealing off the vessels, you prevent the bad humours from reaching the site of injury."

"Huh... I always thought warmth sped up healing," Mothy answered. "Oh! Drua! I saw someone move in there, too."

"Don't encourage her. She'll have to stop making up stories before she joins us in medicine," the brother, Merris, sneered.

"No, really. Look! Someone is in there."

The two goats rumbled up the road, and Sangur jumped down from the wagon with a grin. "Don't look too long. And definitely don't sit too close. The Winter fae are typically unseelie and won't hesitate to snatch you up."

Wolflock stopped walking towards the portal and glanced to Ms Vuori and Lija for confirmation. Lija smiled and tugged his sleeve so she could whisper in his ear.

"He's only joking. The Winter court has a deal to never harm the people in Mystentine city or the university for ever and ever. Fairies can't tell a lie."

Wolflock sighed with dramatic relief. "Thank goodness for that."

"Don't go into the portal though," Ms Vuori warned loud enough for Drua to hear. "The Winter Court time moves more slowly than here. You could go in there for a minute and come out a year later."

Everyone leaped away from the portal and stayed well clear of it, except Lija, who threw snowballs into it while the others prepared lunch.

Wolflock tried to get Mothy's attention again, but he remained firmly engrossed in his medical conversations with Merris. As the company finished their lunch platters of fruits, meats and cheeses, the Vuori ladies and Dr Växtadlare bid everyone merry part and a good trip. Lija hugged Wolflock and Mothy once more and waved as she departed with her mother and the doctor.

Wolflock watched them go back down the road, grateful for the chatter behind him that he didn't have to partake in. Blayne boasted loudly that he already had several literary awards under his belt, but only Drua and Shĭmìsī paid him any heed. Seizing his chance, he plonked himself down next to Mothy, interrupting his conversation.

"It has been a lovely day. What a pleasant stroll. Did you see the strange footprints in the snow, Mothy? I wonder if there are many goblins on the mountain."

Mothy stuffed his mouth full of ice-apple and couldn't respond.

"On the mountain? Not so much, but in the mountain, yes indeed," Merris sniffed, setting down the tea Urgi had boiled for them.

"In the mountain?"

"Oh, that's right. You're new, too. I don't believe we've had the pleasure. Etienne Merris."

"Wolflock Felen." He nodded. "You said something about goblins in the mountain?"

"Ah, yes. Yes. There are cave goblins. They're meant to be some kind of highly intellectual society that is said to guard the soul of the ancient blue dragon. I've only seen them when they become official students at the university. They normally only last a semester or so before they're called away again."

Wolflock pretended to chew the seeds he took up for longer than he needed. He thought Blayne was a terrible boast, but Etienne had an even thicker layer of contempt dripping off him as he spoke. His nasally voice seemed to be stuck in his head just as much as his ego was and, although he addressed Mothy in a mentoring fashion, he made it very clear he had no time for Wolflock at all.

His sister poured her attention on Blayne, who

revelled in it. It had been such a long time since he'd been around people his own age that Wolflock forgot how irritating they could be. Finally, Urgi and Sangur packed up the lunches, made an offering to the Winter portal, and the company began the second half of their walk for the day.

Wolflock stayed in step with Mothy, catching him before Etienne could join them.

"I feel like I haven't seen you for two days. What are your thoughts on your new doctor friend?"

"He's fine," Mothy shrugged, watching the trees on the opposite side of the road.

"I bet you're smarter than him. You've probably had more practical experience than him, anyway."

Mothy didn't respond.

"The mention of goblins made me think that there may be dragons and other beings at the university. It will be so fascinating to meet them. There are a lot of them in Plugh, but father never used to let Myna or I go out much, so I didn't get the opportunity to observe them."

Again, Mothy didn't respond.

Wolflock frowned. "Mothy? Are you well? We're on our way now. You don't have to be nervous anymore. Every step takes us closer to our goal."

"Mmm hmm," Mothy scratched the back of his

neck. His eyes were still a dark shade of furious brown.

"Mothy?"

Wolflock blinked and jerked back as his friend's flaming brown eyes fixed on him. He'd never seen that colour in Mothy's smiling face before.

"I'm fine, Wolflock. Really. I'm just keen to get to the top of the mountain." He ran his fingers through his hair and dropped his hand to his side, grasping his bag strap. "I'm going to ask Etienne about the medical training the school offers."

Wolflock felt his heart freeze.

Mothy had lied to him. At least twice in a few seconds. He was furious about something. But all of that wouldn't have bothered him if not for one thing.

Mothy never called him by his name.

Wolflock stared wide eyed at the ground as Mothy stepped back in line with Etienne and his sister.

What had happened to his friend in the last two days? All he knew was that he wasn't stopping until he found out.

Rhiannon D. Elton

CHAPTER 2

Brown Eyes, Painful Lies

The direct approach was always Wolflock's favourite. It worked once every six times, on average, and even more if the person was too shocked to think of a lie. Most people forget they can refuse to offer any information at all.

"Mothy, what's bothering you?" He charged up to Mothy and cut him off before he could resume his conversation with Merris and his sister. "You've been upset since we woke up this morning and I can tell when you lie."

Mothy glared at him with those burning brown eyes

that were nearly turning black. His hands balled into fists, shaking by his side. For a tense moment, Wolflock thought he was going to hit him.

"I'm fine, Wolflock. Go and make some new friends. Etienne," he turned back to the taller red-haired man, "how would you go about treating a ringworm condition?"

Wolflock felt as if he'd been stabbed. New friends? But he didn't want new friends. He wanted his best friend to smile and laugh and cause mischief with him. He wanted that doting look to tell him how marvellous his intellect was. Wolflock wanted Mothy to build on the framework of their general pandemonium and for them to make even more memories.

If Mothy hadn't been so engrossed in his lunch, they may have discovered new things about the Winter fae portal, or found curious creatures lurking amongst the trees. They might have seen pixies or snow beasts or a goblin. He'd even settle for a deer. But it wasn't just his lunch that Mothy had been engrossed with. It was Etienne.

"Well," Etienne crossed his arms and tapped his chin in thought, "you have to find the edge of the worm and, very carefully, tug it out. Otherwise, they lay more eggs."

"But isn't ringworm a fungal infection?"

"Oh no." Etienne shook his head with a mocking superiority. "Definitely not. That's what the lay folk think, but a doctor knows better."

While Miss Merris looked up at her brother with the utmost admiration, Wolflock noticed that Mothy agreed verbally, but with a twitch in the side of his mouth that said he didn't really concur.

Wolflock frowned even more. If he knew Mothy didn't agree with him, they discussed it. Why was his best friend avoiding him and talking to someone he couldn't even be honest with? Was he just going to pass off Wolflock like discarded ash from a pipe? Had he burnt out the enjoyment they had? He never thought Mothy could be so ruthlessly ambitious.

No. It was Etienne. He had to find someone Etienne would be distracted by and then Mothy would be friendly to him again. His mind blew about his new subject like the snow flurry that sent flakes of ice around them in the breeze.

Etienne stood taller than everyone except for Sangur and Thuthukta. Lanky with a long, oval face and even longer forehead, his flat eyebrows and mouth made his expression look perpetually cold. He donned powdery blue, leather gloves that matched his full-length coat. The thick wool hat he wore didn't match his coat and gloves, which told Wolflock he hadn't planned ahead for the weather, or he didn't have the money for a fully matching set. A family tailor would have created the entire set, knowing the weather it was going to endure, and taken pride in presenting their work to the world.

Wolflock ignored the fact that he was also underdressed, as it was merely because he hadn't given his tailor time to prepare anything. A week was not long enough to make the garments, let alone ship them, so, in this, he excused himself.

The red-haired man waffled on about the patients he'd treated over the Summer, and his little sister nodded along, confirming everything. Whenever one of the patients expressed any kind of grievance, his sister jumped in to assassinate their character and prove that they didn't know what they were talking about. The longer Wolflock tried to stay in the conversation at all, the more awkward it became. Mothy had clearly dismissed him, and, yet, he lingered. He didn't know how to approach the people he didn't know, and he didn't want to continue speaking with Blayne, but, eventually, the tension grew, and he dropped back beside Sangur.

"Are there any other medical students or lecturers in our party?" he asked the long bearded guide.

"None but is in front of us. Mr Merris is well into his

studies. I've taken him up the mountain three times, now, over the years. Miss Merris came along once for a visitation and signed up for the next year's intake. Following in the footsteps of her family. Dunno the other one," Sangur grunted.

His silky blond beard flowed around his face like a satin river and gleamed in the white midday sunlight. Wolflock had only ever seen that sort of shine on Captain Blutro's beard and ponytail. It dredged up feelings of homesickness for the Silver Ice Hair. In the few months he'd spent on it, the old ship had felt more like home than his father's manor ever had.

"That's Mothy. He... he was travelling with me."

Sangur peered down at Wolflock and chuckled. "Don't fret, boy. You'll make plenty of friends in the university. I hear there's a good six thousand students, now. Around a hundred or so for each course. What are you studying, anyway?"

Wolflock bit his lip. "Uh... I'm not sure."

"After a bit of general studies, then? They do have courses for general life skills, but I can't say they're too applicable for anything south of mid Grothener. They don't get snow further South than that."

"No. I'm not after life skills. I just don't know what course would help me get what I want."

"And what do you want?"

His blue eyes shot to Mothy. His friend had given him the words, but, without him to back him up, they felt foolish. "I want to study to become Puinteyle's best... appraising investigator."

"Ah... an investigator, you say? The private type, I'm guessing. Mystentine University has the best science department on the continent. You might want to take a mix, though. Depending on the work you think you'll be doing, I'd say take a general class for everything, but focus on chemistry, biology and history."

"History?" Wolflock blinked in surprise at the tour guide's keen insight.

"Oh, yes. Nothing's new these days. And history tells us what patterns of human behaviour to watch out for."

"I'll consider it. Do you often give advice to new students?" Wolflock considered that staying with the guide may be the best way to spend the trip while he found out why Mothy was upset.

Sangur smiled. "Only the ones that need it."

Wolflock scoffed. He didn't need advice. He'd find out everything he needed when he got to the top of the mountain. "What's up ahead?"

The guide stroked his beard along his jawline. "We walk for another four hours until we reach the cave at the edge of the woodlands. Then we'll set up camp for the evening."

"Is there anything between here and there? Any places to stop and rest?"

"There's a big boulder for afternoon tea two hours further up. Lots of the first timers like to climb it."

Wolflock's eyes flashed. "Excellent. I'll see you there."

Without another word, he marched ahead, overtaking everyone in the group. Sangur called out for him to stop when he got there, but Wolflock had a plan. He would reach the big rock and feign an injury. Mothy's compassion would make him care for Wolflock's injured ankle and he'd have to speak to him. With the added sympathy for his pain, he'd want to make Wolflock feel better and then he could help his friend resolve whatever was bothering him. Simple, effective, foolproof.

After just under an hour of walking as fast as he could, Wolflock paid more attention to his surroundings. The trees on either side of the road held it together, and the city had built large tunnels that drew the streams from the mountain under the road. The most wildlife he saw were birds and the smell of the city had transformed into pine trees. Many of the trees lining the road had their bark stripped from animals and the tiny claw marks left open gashes for the pine sap to leak from.

He reached what he could surmise was the boulder Sangur had spoken about. A towering grey stone with a perfect slope for climbing, it looked as if it were shaped like a dog looking at the sky. Wolflock climbed it to its peak and saw a magnificent view of the city to his left and the Shiriling wilderness to his front. The old pine forest leading down from the mountain stretched out to the horizon in frosty plains. The road ahead swept them around the back of the mountain and likely joined the one above him by a good hundred feet. Wolflock looked over the edge of the rock and took note of where he should sit in order to pretend he'd hurt his leg. He shoved a heap of snow from the rock and felt quite proud of his staging abilities.

He carefully climbed down and sat next to the pile of fallen snow. Wolflock could say the swelling reduced because of the use of the ice, which would explain why there was very little visible injury. He chuckled to himself about how clever he was as he waited. After what felt like an eternity, he heard voices coming down the lane. Their sound echoed up through the trees and he wondered whether the acoustics dampened the sound going down. He tested a low groan and received no response.

He saw Mothy, Etienne and Miss Merris appear on the path and he rocked forward, scooping up the snow, and held it to his pretend injury. He groaned louder as they came up to him.

"Wolflock?" Mothy frowned down at him. "What happened?"

He couldn't help but notice a cold undertone to Mothy's words.

"I climbed to the top of the rock here and slipped. See the snow? Much less traction than what I imagined. I feel-ack-very foolish."

"Ah!" Etienne knelt down and roughly pulled Wolflock's hands away. This wasn't what he wanted. "Just a sprain by the looks of things. Let me have a look here." He pulled Wolflock's foot up and yanked off the shoe. If he had been in actual pain, it would have been agonising.

"I-Mothy has treated this sort of thing before. Let him do it!" Wolflock protested, but his heart sank as his friend shook his head and walked away. "Mothy?"

"Now, now, Mr Felen. Don't fret. The best thing to do with a sprain is to crack it and release the humours."

The rest of the company arrived and crowded around to watch.

"What's happening here?" Sangur asked.

Wolflock sighed with relief. Surely their guide would get the medical student to stop trying to twist his ankle off.

"And three, two-"

CRACK.

Wolflock gasped, and all colour rushed from his face. Etienne had cracked his ankle, sending the worst pain he'd ever felt up his leg. It felt ten times worse than a cricked neck, and a hundred times worse than being beaten around the head by Chestir. Hot fire rushed up to his hip and he couldn't breathe for half a minute.

"There we are. You'll be right as rain." Etienne stood up and dusted his hands. "Is anyone else feeling unwell?"

The group stepped back away from him as hot tears of pain reached Wolflock's eyes. He scooped up the snow again and pressed it into his ankle, scrunching himself into a ball.

"No, no, no ice on this." The medical student tried to move his hands away.

Wolflock swore at him. "Don't touch me!"

Etienne jumped back and Wolflock heard Blayne laugh, but he didn't care. He could feel his ankle actually swelling under his hands.

"Urgi," Sangur barked, "Go get some comfrey. Etienne, leave the triage to us."

The assistant raced off back to the nearest pipe leading under the road and returned, rolling large rough leaves in her hands to bruise them into a poultice.

"That stuff destroys livers," Etienne huffed, lifting his

nose into the air.

Urgi wrapped the leaves around Wolflock's ankle and pressed his hand. "Only if you eat it, and nothing else, for years," she retorted. "Why on Pelaia did you climb the rock with no one here?" she cooed.

Wolflock looked at Mothy, who avoided looking at him. Urgi followed his gaze and waved the blond boy over.

"Hold this. I'll get the bandages from the wagon."

Mothy sighed and knelt down, wrapping his hands around Wolflock's ankle.

"I... I'm sorry," Wolflock winced as he wriggled his toes.

Mothy's eyes lightened into a hazel colour as he gave his friend a sideways glance.

"I didn't mean to worry you."

Brown again.

"I just don't know what happened to make you so upset. I wanted to talk about it, but I guess you'll be looking after me. You can just tell me when you are ready.

Mothy turned his face to Wolflock and squeezed his ankle hard, then released his hands so fast his fingers cracked. "Did it ever occur to you that we've been travelling together for months and that I might just need some space? Haven't we been through enough? Why do you have to keep heaping more issues on me? And, no. I won't be looking after you. The guides are paid for that. Not me."

His best friend shoved himself to his feet and rounded the boulder out of sight. His words burned into Wolflock's mind. Mothy had always seemed to enjoy his company, even favoured him. Had it all been a farce? Was Wolflock just a means to an end? Had their journey and adventures been too much for Mothy to bear?

Wolflock didn't eat afternoon tea and, when everything had been repacked, he had to sit in the back of the wagon until his ankle felt better. Urgi bound it with more comfrey and a spicy paste. Blayne volunteered to sit in the wagon with the melancholy boy and make sure his ankle didn't get worse. Wolflock would have preferred anyone else. Except Etienne.

For another three hours, he listened to Blayne complain about how he had snuck onto the wagon after lunch, as the only decent conversation had crept away. His snide comments about Wolflock, Mothy, the other party members and anyone else Blayne had met went right over Wolflock's head as he watched the back of the road with his leg elevated on a tent bag. He remembered Blayne saying that the only good conversation he'd had was with the wagon. Wolflock took that to mean the goats had chatted with him and he smiled as he thought they were at Blayne's intelligence level.

He laid on the hard wood wagon with his hands folded over his stomach, not saying a word. He thought that, if he didn't respond, Blayne would stop talking, but the dolt took his silence for acquiescence and spoke constantly. Even after they stopped in the clearing they were to set up camp in, Blayne kept on talking for another two hours.

At least he didn't have to watch Etienne and Mothy becoming good friends. The mere thought of that churned his gut, and he decided that he firmly hated the red-haired medical student more than he'd hated anyone.

As the sun set, bringing a blanket of chill over them, Urgi lit the campfire and started dinner while Sangur helped the party set up the six two bed tents and bedrolls.

Wolflock sat on the wagon and watched as the people divided into pairs. Thuthukta the frightening professor and Tareq the business student with the golden turban. Ms Pakuna, the new teacher and Shĭmìsī, the dainty toed food enthusiast. Miss Drua Merris and Fiddi, the engineering student. Mr Terrible-doctor-Etienne Merris and Mothy, and Wolflock and Blayne were last. Urgi and Sangur set up their tent first as an example.

By the time Urgi and Sangur had cooked dinner, the sun had gone to sleep early, and the sky wrapped them in a blanket of stars. Wolflock's ankle felt significantly better thanks to the poultice, and he could walk on it without pain.

Urgi encouraged him to keep it on for the next two days, just to make sure it fully healed.

He hoped to skip dinner and crawl into his tent, when he saw Blayne hadn't started putting it up. Instead, the arrogant boy sat by the fire expectantly for dinner.

"Blayne. Come along. Help me put this thing up."

From behind, Blayne had a similar hair cut and colour to Mothy, and Wolflock half expected to see the smiling face turn and ask him what animal shape or palace should they model their tent after. Instead, he was met with a snide contempt.

"Off you go, then."

"Pardon?"

Blayne laughed. "I'm sorry. Are you deaf as well as stupid? I said go and put it up then."

"It's... it's a two-person job."

"Correction. It's a two-servant job. Do I look like a servant?"

Sangur stirred the frying vegetables, rolling his eyes. "Go help or you'll get no food. Rule number five. Shelter first."

"Yes, yes, yes," Blayne groaned, heaving himself to his feet as if it were the hardest thing in the world. "Or we freeze to death and you won't find us until Spring. Fine. Make this fast, Felen. Come on. Chop, chop. I don't have all day."

Wolflock wanted to throw something in his face, but, instead, took out his frustration on the knots needed to tie the tent down. Although Blayne dragged himself over to where they were told to pitch their tent, he may as well have stayed by the cooking pit. He leaned against the tree and shouted orders at Wolflock, and, when he handled the poles to put up the tent, he did it wrong. Eventually, Wolflock gave up and tried to affix the ropes and canvas in a way to compensate for Blayne's 'help'. By the end of it, he felt quite proud of his resourcefulness. It didn't look neat like everyone else's, but it looked like it would hold up through the night. And the tree next to them helped more than Blayne.

Urgi let the giant goats munch on the remaining grass and Wolflock tested his ankle by walking around the perimeter of the clearing. The bear cave Sangur had mentioned earlier was long deserted, but, as he drew near, a howling wind blew from within.

"Ah! Beware the mountain's monster, Mr Felen," he called.

"What's that?" Drua gasped, tucking her bowl to her chest and causing Urgi to drop a spoonful of vegetables on the ground.

Wolflock made his way over to the fire pit and sat

next to Fiddi.

"Long ago," Sangur grinned, lowering his gruff voice dramatically, "travellers had to only traverse the mountain with the escort of guards. Not for bandits or rogues, but for the threat of the monsters that would snatch them up. Over time, the people of Mystentine made clear paths and wards to keep themselves safe. This worked for certain things, but not for the terrifying fjallarugal."

Drua gasped again and Wolflock was glad to see Fiddi roll her eyes along with him.

"Said to be an invisible monster that lurks in the snow, it waits for unwary travellers to get lost off the path before it snatches them up, never to be found."

"Mmmm. A terrifying thing it is indeed," Urgi smirked as she finished serving dinner. "Tell them about the time it had you cornered, Sangur."

"Oh, I'm sure they don't need to hear that." He waved his hand, waiting for his audience to beg for the story.

"Please tell us," Drua squeaked, her brown eyes as wide as dinner plates.

A few more of the company nodded, eager for the tale.

"I had lost one of my party in a snowstorm, but I used my compass to lead me right to them. We bunkered down under the snow to keep warm, when something heavy walked around us. The fjallarugal sniffed us out in a snowstorm, but it couldn't find us under the snow. Or, so we thought. It started digging with mighty claws as long as my arm. I could hear it getting closer," he dropped his voice, "and closer."

Ms Pakuna and Drua gulped.

"Then it cut through the snow."

"And you saw it?" Drua screamed.

"No. I only saw the white of the snow. But I heard it. I sure did. A long, high scream shook the mountain, and the snow crashed down around us. The fjallarugal lost its prey, but me and the lost student had a solid shelter for the night, and followed the tunnel it dug for itself to the surface in the morning once the storm had passed."

A collective sigh of relief flowed over the party as they finished their meals. Wolflock had never heard of such a creature, but he would love to learn more about it and the folklore at the university.

"Was there any trace of it the next morning?" Fiddi asked, brushing her dark brown hair behind her ear.

"Nothing. Except for footprints."

"What did the footprints look like?" Wolflock asked, automatically taking out his journal to sketch a picture of the interpretation.

"Like the three-toed feet of a dragon."

Or a bird, Wolflock thought, jotting down the story.

As he finished, Fiddi looked over his shoulder. "Are you going into biology?"

"Hmm? Oh. No. Maybe. This is my journal. I..." he paused. He took notes of all the crimes and clues he thought may help his studies. They were so close, and, yet, it didn't feel like a victory. Not with Mothy ignoring him the way he was. "I take notes of the things that I find interesting."

"And what does that involve?" Drua sneered.

It took very little to realise she felt the same contempt her brother had shown for him.

"I'm more observant than the average person. I see things they don't."

"I know what observant means," Drua sniffed.

His eyes flashed in the light of the fire and a smirk crept onto his lips. "Oh, I don't doubt that. I only doubt your ability to apply it."

All eyes turned to Wolflock, wide at his impertinence.

"All I mean is that continuing to defend a terrible medical student in order to potentially get better connections is a fairly unethical way to begin your education. You don't allow a cross word against your brother, even when it comes from himself. Laying it on a bit thick, don't you think? No one idolises their siblings like that. I'm sure your parents pushing you into the medical field was frustrating enough, but to be in your brother's shadow when you know he's incompetent feels like masochism to me. I'm sure your flattery will get you only so far amongst actual educated individuals, but you will have to open a book besides the romance novels you brought with you. Judging by the shape of your pockets and bag, you definitely cleared out your stash from your home in order to protect them from overbearing parents, but they must be heavy hiking them up a mountain. Only someone feeling guilty about bringing them along would hide them on her person like you've done."

Everyone around the fire sat in awkward silence except for Blayne, who laughed.

"Ah! I knew you had some fight in you. Go on. Do another one."

Drua seemed even more offended that Blayne had laughed at her, but his encouragement turned Wolflock's mood sour. No one around the fire wanted him to speak. Especially Mothy. He took up his bowl and left, feeling worse for snapping at the girl. The washing tub sat in the wagon's shadow.

He washed his bowl and fork as anger bubbled up

within him.

He could have uncovered all kinds of secrets about them if he'd looked for a few moments longer, but he didn't. Mothy taught him to be nice to people and now look where he was. Friendless, scrubbing his own dish in the darkness, and he didn't even know why. He threw his dish into the clean try on the back of the wagon, making a loud clattering sound.

"Oi! Get away from there!" Sangur shouted.

Wolflock looked around for what he could have possibly done to upset the guide when he heard a crate creak closed.

"I was only-" Shĭmìsī started from the other side of the wagon.

"No excuses. You can't grab any more food. You can eat all you like on the last day, but not before."

"I was only getting some ginger-"

"You're on dish duty now. I said no excuses."

Wolflock looked under the wagon to see Shĭmìsī huff as she stomped away. He wondered what other spices she brought with her, hopefully for something with a bit of tang. As he made his way around the wagon into the light, he heard another crate creak.

"If you tell me what you have to make these boring meals tasty, I'll cover for you coming back here," Wolflock smirked, thinking Shĭmìsī had doubled back.

His smirk dropped into a frown as he received no response.

He turned to look into the darkness over the back of the wagon and saw a tall figure in the shadows staring right at him. He made out a bald head and high collar. In what little light cut around the mound of boxes in the wagon, Wolflock saw the glint of a twisted knife.

It shook with raging fury in the person's hand.

Wolflock opened his mouth to yell out as the figure stepped forward, still shrouded in darkness. Suddenly, he flinched as a piercing scream shattered the quiet night air. A gust of wind blew through the camp, blasting snow in Wolflock's face, and, by the time he opened his eyes, the figure was gone.

He spun around on the spot, but they were nowhere to be seen. Had it been his imagination?

He heard Sangur tell everyone to get to bed before the fjallarugal came to get them, but his eyes squinted into the darkness.

A hand grabbed his shoulder, and Wolflock jumped in the air with a start. Blayne laughed at him.

"I thought I'd find you and make sure you got to bed safely. Can't have my tent putter-upperer freeze to death til Spring and whatnot."

Wolflock collected himself and frowned once more into the darkness.

"Come along, Felen. What kind of travelling partner would I be if I let you be scared in the night?"

CHAPTER 3

A Dead Man Needs No Compass

Wolflock didn't know what he dreamt about in that stuffy little tent and musty old bedroll. He just remembered an ear-piercing scream. It was unnatural. Just as he thought so, though, it became more natural. Like a man shouting, instead. His body went rigid and his eyes snapped open.

The scream persisted. But it wasn't the fjallarugal's scream. It was someone just outside the camp. Wolflock pulled his dressing gown on and his shoes over his night socks, and pulled back the tent flap. Blayne slept soundly in his own bedroll until the expertly constructed tent crumpled in on him. Wolflock escaped before he could be tangled in it and moved to where he thought the man's scream had come from. He heard Blayne grunting as he thrashed his way out, but he didn't want to let anyone know he'd heard the shout.

He moved towards the cave in the darkness, following the path between the mounds of snow to avoid making a sound. The dark sky's Eastern hem was tinged with grey as the sun slowly rose from its slumber, but the path to the cave was still terribly dark. Wolflock approached the edge of the cave and saw a hole allowing starlight through. He couldn't hear movement or breath.

He held his own and stepped in.

Something behind him grabbed his shoulder, and he jumped a foot in the air, spinning about.

"Blayne!" he hissed, seeing the blond boy in his silky nightcap.

"What did you do? Our tent is ruined! I was having the most wonderful dream about-"

"Shhh!" Wolflock covered the annoying boy's mouth. "I heard someone yell. There may be danger. Shut. Up."

Blayne glared at him and rolled his eyes, but kept

his mouth shut in a pout.

They travelled further into the cave, but it was too dark to see anything at all. Wolflock listened for another moment, unable to hear anything at all, then struck his bone match to cast a grey light around the room.

Blayne gasped, but not at the light. Wolflock and him both saw the man laying on his back, eyes staring into nothing up through the skylight in the cave.

"Is he...?" Blayne whispered.

Wolflock moved forward and knelt beside the frozen figure. "Dead."

He looked around, holding a hand up to Blayne to get him to hold still. The dead man wore a simple, long-sleeved shirt, skivvy shorts, and shoes without socks. He also wore a long pair of blacksmith gloves. Wolflock reached out and touched his patchy, blond bearded cheek. He was still warm. The wispy hairs looked rubbed away, as if he always wore a mask, the same way a sock may cause sparse leg hair. Sparse patches of hair covered his scalp, but there also seemed to be a strange mark on the back of his head. Wolflock turned the man's head and saw a rough, oval patch of redness.

"That's disgusting," Blayne grimaced. "Is... did someone hit him in the back of the head? Was that what killed him?" he asked, twisting his nightcap in his hands.

"No. This is very superficial. It's like an item was pressed here. Like a coin under the rim of a hat. That is what killed him, no doubt," Wolflock pointed to his chest where a small patch of wet blood soaked a palm sized area over his heart.

Blood soaked the back of the shirt. Wolflock could see the tear in the front of his shirt had three distinct lines cut in the fabric.

"He was stabbed from behind by a very long knife with three blades," Wolflock said darkly. "There's a larger pool of blood at his back, and yet the knife went all the way through to his shirt. It's a long knife indeed. Blayne, can you see any clothes around? He couldn't have come here in these. He would have frozen."

"N-no. Clothes? No. Nothing."

"Keep looking. And, if you find any footprints, tell me."

Blayne wandered around the areas of the cave as Wolflock's match lit up, muttering, "I can't believe you touched a dead man."

Wolflock ignored him. The man's skin looked tanned on his face around the beard lines. Had he recently lost it? There were no marks on his arms, further confirming he had been stabbed in the back. Behind him, Blayne collected large white feathers and fanned himself to calm down.

The man looked oddly familiar, but Wolflock couldn't make out why. Did he look like most of the Shiriling men? Perhaps Sangur knew him. He looked down at the man's hands and saw the large blacksmith gloves again. Such an odd item for a man who was barely dressed. Was he a mountain dweller? He hadn't heard of anyone living on the mountain. He reached down to peel the glove back and see if his hands were that of a blacksmith as Blayne circled around to the man's head.

"Oh, ho! What's this?" he scooped up a pendant from the floor. "It's one of our compasses."

Wolflock's face snapped up. "What?" He took two steps up to Blayne and snatched the compass from him. The leather cord was older and had been torn from the man. The compass was much older than theirs. Was this a long-lost traveller?

Wolflock flipped it over and saw a different sigil than what was on his own. More intricate, older, and with an inscription that looked like Shirth, but he couldn't make it out.

"What? Can't read old Shirth? I thought everyone could read old Shirth. I guess only the best educations can do what you want to do."

Wolflock scowled, not wanting to relinquish the

compass.

"Well, go on then. Hand it over."

"I can read it. I just know more of the Southern ancient languages. It will take me a few moments to-"

Blayne tried to snatch the compass back, but Wolflock kept his grip on it.

"Shove off!"

"No! Let me look! Give it here!"

"Blayne! Cut it out!"

Wolflock and Blayne scrabbled over the compass, falling to the dusty floor. Blayne managed to wrestle the compass off Wolflock, raising it with a triumphant, "Aha!"

Wolflock's eyes caught a glimpse of something unnaturally square in the dirt.

"I told you to look for footprints!" Wolflock snarled, shoving Blayne off. He shook his head at the destroyed evidence.

"How was I supposed to see anything I couldn't trip over in the dark? You had the light." Blayne scowled.

A hand reached forward in the darkness behind him and snatched the compass from him.

"What's going on here?"

Sangur's gruff voice sounded more raspy and tired than earlier that day. The guide's grey eyes fell over the body in the darkness. He had a blanket wrapped around his shoulders and, with a flick, he whipped it off and laid it over the man.

"Don't look into the eyes of the dead. It's bad luck."

"Someone killed him with a knife with three blades twisted together," Wolflock frowned, stepping forward to present the case, gesturing to the lines in the shirt coming out in a triangular pattern.

Sangur frowned down at the body under the blanket as he pulled his furry hat down over his ears and eyebrows. "The people on the mountain often live by more savage rules. Never heard of a three bladed knife, but, whenever they get into a scuff, it's before Winter when things get scarce."

"But he had that compass that we have." Wolflock pointed to the necklace Sangur pocketed.

"Oh, you can get these anywhere. Everyone going up the mountain has one. He could have gotten it from any traveller. Help me keep the others back. You've woken all the sleepers up."

Blayne and Wolflock both groaned.

"Now!" barked Sangur.

They raced to the edge of the cave, the bright grey sky growing above the trees. Wolflock scanned the confused and curious faces.

"Wait here, people." Blayne lifted his hands and blocked the path. "Orders of the master guide. Just a dead hobo."

Wolflock's mouth opened in revulsion. "Excuse me! It's a dead man. Don't be so disrespectful."

"What? He's dead. He doesn't need any more respect. The most we can do is bury him."

Wolflock took a long, deep breath to stop himself from throttling the ignorant imbecile.

Sangur came up behind them. "Urgi, go and get a flare. We need the authorities."

"Yes, sir." Urgi nodded, running her fingers over her messy braids as she ran to the wagon.

"Everyone, start packing up. We need to go back to the city."

All at once, the entire company protested loudly. Sangur heaved a sigh. "A man is dead, people."

"He's not one of our people, though," Etienne sneered.

"Just call the authorities and let them come to collect him," Drua followed him up, as was to be expected.

"If you won't guide us to the university, we're just going to go anyway and ask Ms Vuori for a refund with compensation," Blayne chuckled. Wolflock clenched his fists. He wouldn't let anyone hurt the Vuori's like that.

Urgi returned with the flare and pushed her way to the front of the crowd. "What now, sir?"

Sangur looked around the furious group and sighed. "Urgi, you stay here. Send up the flare and wait. The Guard should be along soon. Don't touch him. We don't want to destroy any information they can get from him. Maybe they'll know who he is."

Wolflock's mouth twitched in irritation as he thought about how flicking the blanket over the body had blown away the footprints around him. He also thought it would have been prudent to tell the others about the compass, and he wasn't sure why Sangur left out that detail.

"Very well. You'll all have your way. We will continue on and Urgi will wait here for them. Catch up with us if you have time."

"Yes, sir. I'll take the back trails and meet you at the third day's lunch stop."

Sangur nodded, ushering everyone back from the cave as Urgi lit the top of the flare. A stream of flaming red sparks released into the air and a series of whizzing explosions launched high into the morning sky.

The crowd started moving away, but Wolflock

missed the face he wanted to see most. The only other one who knew about the twisted knife.

"Mothy?" Wolflock frowned. If the person with the twisted knife was nearby, that meant that Mothy was in just as much danger as him. "Mothy!" He shouted.

He only received more confused looks. Wolflock took off like a rabbit to Mothy's tent. He dived down to throw open the tent flap, but his head collided with something hard, and he fell back onto the wet grass.

"Wolflock? What the he-"

Mothy caught himself, and his cheeks flushed red. Even in the sparks from their head collision, Wolflock could tell Mothy had slept poorly and was about to use a turn of phrase he would rather not.

"Thank the gods you're safe. Mothy! The knife! The man with the curved knife! He's here."

Mothy scowled, rubbing his head. "Sure."

"What?"

"I'm sure they are. Is this why you've woken everyone up?"

"Mothy, someone is dead!" Wolflock couldn't believe it.

Mothy's brown eyes seemed to have stone grey flecks in them. "Let the guides deal with it."

"I can't believe you right now! Listen, if you won't

talk to me, I won't pretend to know why, but solving who killed this man is the only way we'll be safe from him. Everyone here is at risk."

"Why won't I talk to you? Ha!" Mothy snarled bitterly. "You're the smart one. Go figure it out. Just stay away from me."

Wolflock glared at him, and, with a growl, turned on his heel and stalked away.

Rhiannon D. Elton

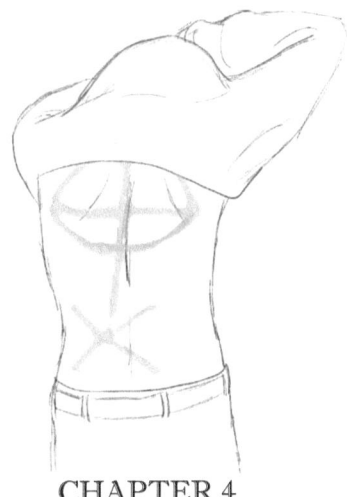

CHAPTER 4
Waiting, Watching

In order to help with the journey ahead and Urgi's impending absence, Sangur had her instruct Fiddi on how to manage the giant goats, and Shĭmìsī became their new chef. Wolflock remained in such a volatile mood that Blayne didn't argue when he snapped at him to help pack the tent up. Not that he helped. The obnoxious rich boy tried to cram everything into the pack without folding the canvas or aligning the poles. He even wrapped the rope up in a terrible ball that Wolflock did not look forward to untangling later.

They were the last to finish packing their things and, to make sure Wolflock's ankle didn't get worse, Sangur told him to stay on the wagon for the first half of the day with a fresh poultice. He felt fine, but he didn't mind being separated from the rest of the group. He couldn't guarantee he would be able to maintain the civilities Mothy brought out of him while they were at odds.

Thinking of Mothy stung worse than his ankle and he spent the first half of the day hugging his good leg to his chest, watching the road behind them while Blayne drawled on about how wealthy his family was and how well connected they were. Wolflock wished he could refute it the same way he'd done to Etienne's sister last night, but his brief observations of Mr Amery Blayne told him the boy was honest. Obnoxious, arrogant, and small-minded, but wealthy and well connected.

The same as the Thorns, Wolflock thought to himself as he tried to tune out Blayne's inane bragging.

"Are you still upset about your servant throwing a spat at you? That's what happens when you pay them too much. You'd be better off spending it on getting that vest fixed. The embroidery is frayed."

Wolflock blinked lazily and moved his eyes onto Blayne's sneering face without moving any other part of his body. "He's not my servant. I don't pay him. He's my friend."

"Yes, yes. I have those too. Layabouts who like to spend my money for a good time and leave you high and dry when you run out of allowance." Blayne waved him off.

Wolflock usually knew better than to argue, but his sour mood dissolved his self-control. "Mothy pays for all his own things," he lied. It didn't feel like a complete lie, though. Mothy never wanted him to pay for anything, and he budgeted enough to get by.

"Is that why he's mad at you? Go on. Give me the gossip. I thought having to ascend the mountain in such a rustic fashion would be the ultimate equaliser of peoples."

"He's not mad at me over money. He's mad at me because..." Wolflock trailed off. Why was Mothy upset?

They had saved Lija from capture. Mothy rushed in to stop Chestir from beating Wolflock to a pulp, and then he woke up. His friend had been relieved and happy to see him and helped him downstairs to explain the case to Captain Estivan and the Vuori ladies. Was it something in the explanation that upset him? Did he not give Mothy enough credit?

Wolflock's lips pulled taut as he thought.

Blayne leaned forward expectantly, then huffed and smacked the wood of the wagon floor. "You do realise that your friendship with that boy is completely beneath you? What can he possibly offer you? It's a very one-sided arrangement, as far as I can see."

Wolflock looked at Blayne as the sheer offence of that statement wracked through him. "Mothy has always given me beyond what I have ever hoped. When we first met, he was the one who showed me all the secret places over the ship. He saved my hide more than once, and he's one of the most entertaining people I've ever met. He's clever, capable, and has more life experience than either of our entire families for generations."

"What did you do, then? If he's such a stand up gentleman, what heinous crime have you committed to lose his affection?" Blayne sneered with acid in his tone.

Wolflock turned away. He couldn't look at Blayne and think straight. What was Mothy sensitive about? His past. His parentage. Slavery. Children in danger. Wolflock hadn't stepped on any of those ills, though. He knew better than to even tease his friend on such topics.

He gripped his black hair and groaned. "I don't know. If I knew, I'd fix it and we wouldn't be having this conversation."

"Well, my old pa used to say to count your

blessings. At least he's alive to try and reconcile with. Unlike that chap from the cave. And, if he won't make it, then good, then you can choose better company."

Wolflock made a face and heaved a sigh.

"Well, you're too melancholy for me to pander to right now. I'll be back after a stroll and you'd best change your attitude, Felen. Else I will reconsider being so kind to you."

He watched the blond boy go, shaking his head. His sheer audacity was enough to leave Wolflock bewildered and furious.

But soon, the deceased man in the cave crept back into his mind. He hadn't realised how loud his thoughts were when he was left alone. He hadn't understood why Sangur had been so clinical in seeing the body. The first time Wolflock even thought he saw a dead body, he'd had a visceral reaction. Perhaps lots of people died on the mountain and he had grown accustomed to it.

The man in the cave hadn't looked malnourished, though. He looked fit with the typical, bulky Shiriling physique. Something about his skin made him look leathery. The mystery man had spent a lot of time in the outdoors, but only around his eyes and nose sported a tan. He'd been clothed. His skin had been warm to the touch. The blood was fresh.

The image of the dark figure with the swirling knife lurked in the back of Wolflock's mind. Who was the dead man and why had the man with the knife killed him? Where was the knife man now?

The compass necklace twisted one of Wolflock's thought-web strands around his gut. Sangur had said they were worthless, but, as he flipped his own over in his hands, he couldn't help but appreciate the antique craftsmanship. And the engraved sigils for protection were not easy to make. Specialised artisans were employed for the task based on their favoured materials. Was the wizened guide trying to stop him from worrying? Or had he lied?

Something was off.

Wolflock climbed on top of the cargo and looked out across the strolling travellers. Suddenly, all of them looked suspicious to him. All of them had something to hide, and one of them may have been a killer.

To keep Mothy safe, he had to find out who.

He didn't know any of them well enough to trust them, and he certainly didn't know what they were capable of. He only knew a man had been murdered, by the same man who tried to kill Parihaan. He remembered the knife gleaming in the darkness of her room. Then there was the note he woke up with after trying the drinking alcohol that led him straight to Parihaan as the smuggler. Wolflock whipped out his journal and found the note folded in the pages.

P.

When you get to Krieger Zwerg, make sure the goods get on board. Someone will meet you in Creast for pick up. The boss will be furious if you drink it all again like last time.

Don't mess up.
A.

He didn't remember finding it. He'd just woken up with it in his hand. Had someone deliberately given him the information he needed to resolve the mystery without finding the mastermind behind it all? That had bothered him for months.

Don't mess up.
A.

It had to be Astraxis, with his toxic flowers and mind controlling powder. He watched as Shĭmìsī tip toed over to the wagon, thinking she remained unobserved, and started looking for things in the crates while it kept moving. He didn't interrupt her. The sneaky, round lady fascinated him. With a cute grin, she lifted out a handful of herbs and slipped them into her pocket before skipping back to Ms Pakuna, who he noticed had a long thin corn pipe on her belt. She passed the lecturer the handful of herbs she'd taken and Ms Pakuna put it into her pipe, but, instead of smoking it, she waved it around both of them like seining incense.

Fiddi began coughing as the thick, sweet-smelling smoke wafted back over the wagon. Even in the open air, it had an overpowering smell. It brought back memories of being cooped up in Bleen and Faleen's cabin for his fortune telling.

The memory made him bite his lip. The horrible sensation of trusting someone with your hopes and dreams, only to have them shattered before you. That scene was forever burned into his mind. The tasselled cushions, the heavy tapestries, the fake trinkets from fake dignitaries. And that awful incense that left everyone in a suggestive stupor.

He recalled seeing the container in their room filled with it. And the note attached to it.

"...and Astraxis can make this into the incense of

your dreams. Love Gilmere."

His gut turned to ice. Of course, the twins had known Astraxis. How else would they have gotten an incense made of herbs that controlled the will of others? But the note suggested the incense hadn't been prepared when they received the package. The only place they could have received post was from the Krieger Zwerg post office. Which meant that Astraxis had to be on the ship to make up the incense for them. He'd been using the Silver Ice Hair crew and company as experiments for his terrible powders.

The loose thread from all of his cases started pulling themselves together. Little things that hadn't made sense at the time now fit into place, and Astraxis was at the core of it all.

He flicked through his journal so ferociously he tore three pages. Right back after Ungul and Uhnha left, when everyone started falling ill from the Tuiti fruit and river bug poisoning, Wolflock had found a handkerchief with the same dried purple sea slug hanging off a barrel. He'd thought nothing of it besides finding a curious trophy. After a nap on the deck, he had heard Grogen vomiting over the side of the ship. He'd been doing laundry. He hadn't been eating. Wolflock remembered thinking that it was odd for one of the jackets to be in the water below.

Astraxis had used his powder on Grogen and made him sick. He practised controlling people by making him throw a laundry item overboard. He'd been right there with Grogen while Wolflock slept on the deck. Then he'd practised on the ship's stew and nearly killed Mothy.

Wolflock forgot to breathe.

What if Mothy was his target all along?

Just days before, Mothy had run around the deck in front of everyone without a shirt on, incidentally showing his scar. Astraxis's goal all along was to establish a slave trafficking cell in Mystentine, so having someone around who knew what that looked like from the inside was dangerous.

He had to move. Wolflock couldn't sit still any longer. He climbed down from the tower of cargo and began pacing in a circle around the wagon as the goats bobbed on.

There was a direct link between Parihaan smuggling the drinking alcohol onboard for A, the sickness that nearly killed his best friend, and the ingredients used to make the Lady Mind Master powder. The only person at the centre of any kind of large-scale criminal activity had to be Astraxis. When she became a danger to his enterprise, he thought to do away with her while she slept in a coma. But Wolflock had gotten in the way.

After that, the fiend had cut Wolflock's lifeline during the storm, which would have drowned him had Himi not saved him. At Creast, they had chased him without knowing, even glimpsing him in Lord Therym's office, as well as the traces of the purple powder used on the captives in the lumber mill shed, the mayor's jacket collar, and in Najord's possession. Volseggir had used the same powder for over a year to numb the minds of Blandt and Maret'Anna. The threads spinning together into Wolflock's mental web were dusted with that wretched purple powder.

He knew Astraxis was definitely a man. He also knew that anyone could be within his connections. The only person he could trust to not be the architect at the centre of all this was the one he wished he didn't have to.

Rhiannon D. Elton

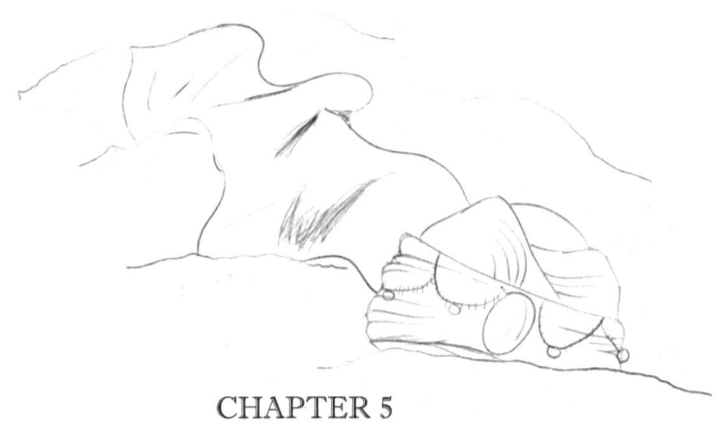

CHAPTER 5

The Impossible Fool

A mery Blayne.

"I can see you're not finished sulking, but at least you're on your feet," the snooty voice smacked him from behind. "Did you discover what it is that you've done to upset the servant boy?"

"Again, he's not a servant." Wolflock pinched the bridge of his nose and stopped pacing. "I do have something I need to talk to you about, though."

"Oh?"

Wolflock dropped his voice and, against his better judgement, told Blayne the truth. "You were the only one

I can confirm was asleep when the man last night was murdered. I can confirm you're not the murderer, but no one else."

"Well, of course I didn't do it!" Blayne laughed loud enough to turn heads to them.

"Shh. Now, listen. I know that's not your strong suit but-"

"Say something interesting and I'll give you the time of day. Until then-"

"I need your help to find the culprit. It's harder to do these sorts of things alone," Wolflock cut over him.

Blayne smirked. "Why not ask the-"

"If you call him a servant again, I'm going to make you set up the tent."

The blond boy winced. "That means you wouldn't sleep in it either."

"For someone who thinks they're well connected, I didn't see you sidling up with the guide master. He and I are friends now. Since Urgi stayed behind, I'll stay in his tent."

Blayne's smirk dropped. "Why should I help?"

Wolflock hadn't considered that Blayne would need a reason to help him besides the thrill of the mystery and serving justice. "Well, the man we're after is at the centre of a significant criminal enterprise, and I suspect he's here to achieve some kind of delivery to the university and make up for the damage we've done. We eliminated a major trading partner for him and alerted the authorities to a slavery industry he was attempting to launch." He cocked his head, proud to announce the significant achievements. "If you help me get him into custody, you'll join the university with an exciting reputation."

Blayne clicked his teeth with his tongue. "I suppose I can spin that tale. You have to milk any excitement for all it's worth. Very well." He held out his hand. "You have a deal."

Wolflock shook his soft hand back and filled him in on the details of what Astraxis had done, the clues left behind, and his possible interactions with him.

"Well, you see, your first problem is that you never told the authorities. The Captain is a legally bound Guardsman, as is his first mate. Sometimes, even the bosun is. You could have given over the evidence at Krieger Zwerg, Irid, Creast and Mystentine, but you didn't. Tut, tut. That would have made this all much easier. We'll tell Sangur first and see what he thinks."

"What? Wait! No. Blayne, stop!" Wolflock gripped his arm and pulled the stubborn boy away from the main throng of people. "What if he's the man we're looking for?"

"Oh, tosh. He came in after we found the body."

"Don't you see? That makes it even more suspicious. And then he covered the body right away, destroying the footprint you had already half ruined."

"Well, excuse me for trying to be helpful. Are you always this suspicious? Who hurt you?"

Wolflock snorted as the group pulled into a rocky plateau overlooking the city. It was nothing more than a grey smear amongst the phthalo forests below them. They were so high he thought he could glimpse the ocean miles away to the West. Fiddi tended to the goats, letting them munch on the bushes away from the cliff side of the road. One started climbing the vertical cliff as if it could ignore gravity.

"I saw Shĭmìsī taking herbs out of the wagon and Sangur caught her trying to get extra food and spices last night. I think we should start-"

"Nonsense. She's just a hungry heifer. It's Fiddi you need to watch out for. Watch." Wolflock opened his mouth in outrage at how Blayne spoke about Shĭmìsī, but the sheer stupidity of the boy left him speechless. "Oh, Miss Fiddi."

The dark-haired girl wobbled a goat's flubbery neck before looking right at Blayne. Wolflock didn't know how Blayne kept his nerve. Fiddi's fiery brown eyes heard the same note of insolence and her stiff presence commanded the whole road. Even the goats watched her, slowly chewing the leaves of the bushes.

"Have you noticed anything strange going on in the last few days? Strange people? Using strange substances? Wielding strange knives? Perhaps less attractive people than myself, but with similar hair colours?" Blayne squinted blatantly at Mothy.

Wolflock slapped his forehead and looked around. His anxiety grew as he saw everyone watching the spectacle. Fiddi didn't answer Blayne. She just looked him up and down with a pointedly raised dark eyebrow.

"Because my friend here thinks that his new nemesis is colluding with a criminal mastermind, but I know that the only master of anyone's mind is you."

Fiddi scoffed and Wolflock stepped back, wishing he could evaporate to get away from whatever Blayne was thinking.

"And what crime have I committed?" Fiddi asked.

Sangur awkwardly made his way around the back of the wagon to help Shĭmìsī get the materials for lunch.

"One of the heart." Blayne knelt down on one knee in front of the short woman.

"Excuse me?"

"No!" Drua screamed from behind the crowd of people.

"Aha!" The blond boy hopped back to his feet and pointed to Drua. "I knew it!"

Wolflock couldn't bear it anymore. He grabbed Blayne's arm and hauled him along the road, away from everyone. As he looked back to apologise, but saw Mothy's disgusted expression and couldn't summon the words. He turned away and pulled Blayne away as he shouted back something about him being the most alluring man there.

He couldn't believe it had taken him less than a minute to completely destroy the frail plan Wolflock had concocted. Frustration and fury burned through every vein of his body. He wished he had it in him to be violent and started considering that this was how people felt when they said he'd benefit from a good slap. All he could muster was to shove Blayne down onto a flat rock now that they were out of sight of the party. He pinched the bridge of his nose and took long, deep breaths to calm down.

"I knew it all along. I'm a genius. You can thank me now, if you like. Granted, it's more to my benefit now that I know." Blayne sat smugly with his arms folded on the rock.

Never had Wolflock wanted to strike someone as much as Amery Blayne. He was even more infuriating than his little sister.

"You can ask any moment, now."

Wolflock gritted his teeth. "I want to ask what you were possibly thinking. How was any of that going to help me-"

"Help us."

"-catch a killer? You've not only alerted Astraxis to my plans-"

"Our plans."

"-but you've compromised my whole investigation-"

"Our entire investigation."

"-you've insulted possible witnesses and people who could help me, but I draw the line at you falsely accusing my best friend to spur on some imagined love triangle with a woman who is not interested in you, and another who doesn't know better!"

Blayne's smile didn't waiver for a moment. "Feel better? Very good! My turn."

Wolflock felt his brain snap from whiplash. For the third time, Blayne had left him speechless.

"Ever since I saw her, I knew she was special, but I didn't know why until just now. See, I knew she wasn't there for the medicine. She's desperate to look up to anyone else, and she didn't realise that I could be that person. That twang of pain plucked her heartstrings, sharp enough to send a note that will reverberate for months. Maybe even years."

Wolflock looked at him blankly. "What are you talking about?"

"Miss Merris!"

The only sound came from the brush brushing down the mountain and ruffling Wolflock's tangled black hair.

This idiot had created some half cocked plan to see if one of the girls in the group liked him. No matter what fancy language he packed around it, Wolflock could only smell the pungent stink of conceit. The only thing he could do was cut himself free and hope Blayne wasn't sticky. Without another word, he turned and walked away. As he made it back to the lunch camp, he ignored the accusatory stares and saw Shǐmìsī had put together a spicy smelling stew. He avoided the communal stew and took up the seed bread instead. He had just been reminded about not eating communal food he hadn't seen cooked.

He pushed against the hostile energy and took a seat on a rock next to Fiddi.

"Merry meet. I don't think we've been officially introduced. I'm Wolflock Felen."

"The appraising investigator. I've heard about you." Her nose twitched. She had a sweet face that hid her commanding energy. The way she held herself made him think she often was the one who was put in charge. "Fiddi Calon. Merry meet."

Wolflock took a bite of his bread without looking at her and swallowed before he spoke again. "If you know about me, you may have gathered what kind of man I am."

He ignored her amused smile.

"I don't apologise flippantly, and I don't apologise for the mistakes others make when in association with me. But I... feel I must make it known that I do not condone Mr Blayne's actions, and he is not my associate."

"And why are you saying this to me? I believe Miss Merris was far more upset by his words than I was." Fiddi turned to Wolflock with a grin that pinched the side of her nose.

"You're smart enough to know I'm being honest. And I can see you're intelligent, organised, and confident in what you do. Which, guessing by the ingenuity of your bracelet that, if I may..." He reached out, and she rested her wrist in his hand. The bracelet had Puinteylien script numbers for various measurements. He unclipped the bracelet, and it snapped into a foot long ruler with extendable pieces that created a protractor, compass and level. "You're an engineer."

"And an architect."

"You're from South Grothener."

"Mid."

"Ah. Dua then. It's warmer South of the Zilber River."

"How did you know I lived in a warmer climate?" She grinned.

"Well, you're rugged up like the Merris siblings, who actually are from South Grothener. You're more tanned than they are and you're used to hot weather. This is your second time coming up to Mystentine university, which is why you're better prepared for the cold than most of us. That would have meant you did the first part of your studies at Shellinden. But you left." Wolflock's voice softened, and he tilted his head to the side. "Why did you leave?"

Fiddi's face split into a grin. "Go on. Guess. This is fun."

Wolflock took a breath and squinted. "Hmm..." She wore very little jewellery, but what she did have on was very well designed. Simple, authentic, yet with just the right flourishes. Her clothes were tailored in an exceptionally practical way. Every stylish inch had pockets and her thick skirt cleverly disguised the fact they were trousers. All of her luggage on the wagon he'd seen was monogrammed, and she had two trunks. One looked similar to Wolflock's clothing trunk, but she also had a flatter, harder case that looked like a specialised toolbox.

"You left Shellinden because they were holding you back. You're good at what you do. Possibly great. You have specialised equipment that's all your own. That tells me that the universities haven't supplied you with what you need to do the best job. You're a practical, forward thinking woman who doesn't let custom hold her back. Did you argue with someone there? It would have to be someone who was at the head of the department and could make decisions over you that you couldn't contest."

Fiddi snickered. "I used to say that, while they walked a donkey, I was trying to fly a dragon."

Wolflock laughed along with her before dropping his voice. "Listen, if you can keep an eye out for anything strange, I'd really appreciate it."

"What kind of strange? And why do you need another set of eyes? Sounds like it could be pretty scary," she teased.

Wolflock's lips pulled flat. "Purple powder, an eye shape with an X through it, drinking alcohol or anything addressed to a man named Astraxis. Anything relating to the dead man and his identity, too."

Fiddi's cheeky smile faded into a thoughtful one, and she nodded slowly. "The only thing I've come across is the new chef getting very excited about some purple flowers she found. I'll keep an eye out for anything else, though." She smacked his arm. "Now get going or Little Mr Blayne will think he has vicarious permission to speak to me again."

"And we definitely don't want that." Wolflock took a sharp inhalation. "I'll be the shield for that onslaught."

"Very gentlemanly, Mr Felen. Merry part."

"And merry meet again."

Wolflock gave her a little bow and walked around the outskirts of the rocky plateau as he thought. It was a good place to pace. The two people high on his list to inspect were Shĭmìsī and Sangur. The guide master had given him good advice, but he couldn't rule out that it was a ruse. He was also the only person in the group that held weapons, and he took the compass from the crime scene. He had to tread more carefully, approaching Sangur to obtain that information.

Shĭmìsī would be easier to confront about why she stole from the wagon and what purple flowers she'd recently acquired. He made up his mind to monopolise her company until he had gotten the answers he needed. The way Blayne kept mocking her made Wolflock hope she was innocent so he could shut the sarcastic fool down.

The company packed up lunch and carried on along the road. Their journey grew steeper and the only things not complaining were the goats. Like mini, moving mountains, it baffled Wolflock how they were able to ignore the restraints of physics. Wolflock's calves regretted that his ankle had healed so quickly. Even Sangur seemed to struggle as they followed the road. So, to give his legs the energy they needed, he kept his head down.

As they made their way over the old dirt roads, the tracks of past carriages faded. Roots reclaimed the compacted earth, and Fiddi navigated the wagon over and around long-standing rocks.

Wolflock looked to the sun, but it was tucked behind the mountain. The cold air told him night was fast approaching. And he felt his gut twist as he wondered when they'd stop to make camp. He huffed and puffed up to Sangur just as the guide master opened his compass and drew out a map.

"Ah! I thought it looked different. We'll make camp just up here where the trees thin."

Wolflock didn't get a chance to speak to him as the party regained some energy from those words. The snow fell lightly around them as they set up their six tents, and a few of the party searched for extra firewood so Shǐmìsī could start dinner before the darkness set in. He seized his chance and caught Shǐmìsī at the back of the wagon.

"Merry meet, can I help?" he said in the same basic Xiayahn Nü had taught him and Mothy.

Shǐmìsī blinked her big, dark eyes at him. "Oh! Haha. No," she giggled. "I'm from the Jaw. That's Eye Xiayahn. You know? Around the lake shaped like a giant eye? I speak perfect Puinteylien, though. It's much easier than dealing with a bad accent."

She waved him off and picked up one of the boxes. With a little shake, she tested its weight and her smile fell.

"Is everyone well?" he asked and picked up the cooking stand.

"Are you going to do the thing where you say secrets very loud and embarrass me?" she whispered rapidly.

Wolflock chuckled. "Do you have embarrassing secrets? Besides arguing with Sangur about taking food."

"I wasn't taking food! I brought my own spices.

Shiriling and Grothener food is so bland. I don't know why you all insist on making it so boring. I only wanted to bring some excitement to it. Grab that bag. I'll show you what I mean."

Wolflock did as he was instructed, and they set up the cooking space. Shĭmìsī also laid out a blanket and opened her large, drawstring bag, which consisted of twelve concentric pockets and one large central space, when completely unfastened.

"Food is like music. If it's boring, it had better be filled with love and goodness. Then it's not boring anymore. I wanted to share my herbs, but, when Sangur accused me of stealing, I felt very salty," she explained as she scooped up fresh snow to melt in the pot. She nodded to the matches and Wolflock tried to start the fire. He eventually got some embers going, but it gave Shĭmìsī the silence she needed to fill.

"I made sure we had plenty of spice and warmth to take away the cold of the mountain, but our big hike today needs lots of good qi to help us build our strength for tomorrow. The potatoes and root plants are fine, but we also need some good miso paste," she scooped out the red soy bean paste and mixed it into the cauldron, "and some seaweed that we'll add at the end. Natural salt is good for building your endurance and kidney energy, but we're using lots of qi getting up the mountain, so a good helping of rice would be wonderful. We'll make do with potatoes, though."

Wolflock found the musical tones in her voice enchanting, and the way she spoke about food made him feel like he could listen to her for hours. Her knowledge and passion shone through brighter than the poorly lit fire, that was for sure.

"There has to be some flavours in Shiriling you like, though," he pushed. "Natural berries, barks or flowers?"

Shǐmìsī bustled and drew a handful of purple berries out from her pocket. "I don't know if these are safe yet, but they looked so juicy. I'm going to ask at the university if they're any good. If they are, I'll grow a little pot of them in the greenhouses."

"That's another class I have to add to my list. Botany is going to help me a lot. What classes are you taking?"

She chortled, putting a hand on her jiggling belly. "Military ethics, of course."

Wolflock coughed. "I... what?"

"That's a joke, silly. I'm going to study food. One day, I want to go to all of the universities and study food. I want to be the first person to combine the best of each country's cuisine and share them."

Wolflock laughed. She had thrown him off and she knew it.

"You didn't have any lunch earlier. I saved you some in my flask if you like."

Wolflock took the flask and sniffed it. "Mothy got very sick last time we ate from a big communal stew, so I'm just a bit cautious. I hope I didn't insult you."

"I just thought you didn't eat much. You're so skinny." She laughed. "Don't worry. They make sure you eat very well at the universities."

Wolflock took a swig of the flask and felt a crackling fire rush through him. He sweat over his scalp and the pure spiciness burnt away any aches and pains from the hike.

"Also, that dish is too spicy to make anyone sick. If you make anything hot enough, it burns away all the bad qi. Then, you finish up with a nice cup of green tea or peppermint to cool back down. We don't need any cooling here, though. Can you believe it's still Autumn, and it's this cold?"

Wolflock took another drink from the bottle and passed it back.

"Grothener is only a bit warmer than this in Winter. We're inland, so there isn't a coastal breeze to warm us up."

"Even the mountains in Shiriling get the ocean weather." Wolflock noted a sigh from her as she spoke about her homeland.

"Do you have family back in Xiayah?" he asked and continued working on the fire.

"Mmm. Yes."

"Do you miss them?"

"Sometimes."

The sadness in her voice filled the air between them, and Wolflock frowned. "I have trouble getting along with my family, too. Two days ago was the first time I'd written to my father in months. We didn't leave on such good terms."

"Oh? Why is that?"

Wolflock sighed. If he was just honest enough, she might tell him what he needed to know. "My father didn't like that I was so observant and outspoken. He wanted us to stay in the shadows, but I have bigger aspirations than just taking over the family business. I have dreams and he got mad that I was still following them, even though he told me not to."

Shǐmìsī's eyes brimmed with tears. "I know that feeling all too well."

"So, this is my chance to prove him wrong. I can

study what I want to and become the person I want to be. You're the same, too, aren't you?"

Wolflock looked up, but saw a rush of black hair and felt himself thrown about like a rag doll. The large Xiayahn woman threw herself forward and hugged him so tightly he thought his bones would break.

"We are kindred spirits!" she sobbed over his shoulder. "There, there. Don't cry. We have each other. My family didn't want me to eat food that wasn't made from our restaurant, and to only eat sushi for the rest of my life!"

He patted her back as best he could, but Wolflock couldn't feel his fingers.

"So I ran away. I ran away and I will never go back. Not for all the promises and prestige in the world. I'm going to make my dreams come true and you should too, my slim friend. You should too." She set him back in his seat and tidied her eyes.

Although his ribs hurt, Wolflock couldn't help but smile. Perhaps it was the spicy food.

"Do you have a special knife set? Any of the chefs I've met are very particular with their knives."

Shǐmìsī nodded and sipped the brewing pot before throwing in another handful of spices. "Yes. But not here. I have them posted to me when I travel. I always keep my special one here, though. She's a good, all round useful one." She plucked out a little paring knife. "It's good for travel."

"Have you ever seen a swirling knife? One with three sides?"

She leaned back and thought, looking up at the sky with the tips of her index fingers pressed into her round chin. "Now that you mention it, I think Tareq had something like that. He has a whole kit of fancy knives. Ceremonial ones he got from Uluken. He said they were some kind of a spiritual gift from a big business he helped. He's studying business ethics, but he's terrible. I've worked in my family's restaurant all my life and we know how to do food as well as business. He said we should throw out the entire menu and make it modern."

Wolflock scoffed with her. "What does that even mean?"

"He didn't know. He just threw around a bunch of buzzy words that confused my old aunt. Poor dumpling."

"Has he been acting strangely? I assume you both came from the pass near Uluken."

"Sure did. We travelled all the way here together. That's how I know he's rubbish at business. Do you think he's the one stealing food?"

Wolflock blinked. "Wasn't that you?"

Shĭmìsī shook her head. Then nodded. "I didn't steal food. I only took spices to make the meals nice. When I checked the crates for lunch, I saw that one had been pried open and emptied. Only the crumbs of seed bread were in the corners."

"You didn't say anything."

"Well... I thought Sangur would blame me. There's no way I could eat that much boring old bread. For me, every bite must breathe something new."

"The box is still on the wagon?"

Shĭmìsī blushed plum. "No. It's... I brought it over here."

"You thought you could pretend we emptied it during this meal and you wouldn't be in trouble, didn't you?"

She nodded, her shoulders creeping up to her ears.

Wolflock examined the box. He ran his hands over the rough cuts in the wood and the splinters around the edge. Someone had tried to pry it open with a thick, hard implement, judging by the grooves left in the wood where leverage had been applied. Whatever it was, it looked like it had a razor edge and formed a broad triangle shape.

"Do you know of any knife or cooking utensil that

is shaped like this?" Wolflock formed his hands into a broad triangle.

Shĭmìsī shook her head. "It could be a strange style spatula, but I only ever use wood unless I'm cutting the ingredients."

"And eating," Wolflock corrected. "A fork or spoon?"

She pinched her earring. He saw the single silver stud had two dangling chains with inch long silver stems. She split the earring between her fingers and gave the stems a flick, springing out nine-inch-long chopsticks with a flash.

"That is very handy," Wolflock smiled, amazed by the smooth silversmithing of the slender sticks.

"It's more versatile than a plain old fork or spoon." She winked at him as she twirled them around her plump fingers.

"I'll have to keep that in mind. Thank you, Shĭmìsī. Is there anything else you need help with?"

"Oh, no. It's an easy dinner tonight. I'll keep your pot separate if you like."

"I would greatly appreciate that. Perhaps don't let anyone but us know, though, yes?"

She nodded to him as he rose and gave her a little bow. He looked around the clearing for Tareq but couldn't see him or his gold glinting turban.

"Ah! I see you've finished chatting with the cook." Blayne slammed his hands down on the back of Wolflock's shoulders, making him jump. "Oh? I startled you? Never mind that. Did you see the way Miss Merris glared at Miss Calon? I told you, didn't I?"

Wolflock swallowed his disgust at the petty gossip. "You wouldn't have seen where Tareq walked off to, would you?"

"Oh, he went to get wood down the little path there when we stopped. I thought as a man of fashion he'd appreciate some idle chatter, but then he baulked at me when I announced myself as a Blayne. Social standing is a weapon as much as it is a curse. Wait, where are you- I told you Mr Shanif went to get wood down that way. He's a big strapping man, he won't need your help, and you'd insult him to offer it. Stay here and play cards with me."

Wolflock stepped away without a second glance until Blayne whined like a child. He clenched his fists and turned around, continuing to walk backwards down the road. "Blayne, I really don't care in the slightest. Go play with Etienne. You're in the same circles."

He turned again and trotted down the path, leaving Blayne to wonder what on Pelaia he meant.

The woods thickened as he crunched the snow

downhill. If Tareq was trying to haul logs up this way, Wolflock did not envy him. The walk itself had been more than enough manual labour for him. He didn't want to add anymore to it. The stubborn evergreens bore the weight of the snow blocking the last of the afternoon sun. The air felt more quiet than Wolflock had ever heard it. His breath misted his vision with fog and he kept a keen ear out for any movement from Tareq.

A clump of snow dropped onto his head, and he brushed it out before it could melt. Just ahead of him, the ground levelled out. Something glinted in the snow. Something gold.

"Tareq? Merry meet?" he called between the silent trees.

"Shh!" hissed a voice by his ankle.

Wolflock jumped back and slipped down the embankment off the path, scraping his chin on the snow. He groaned as he rubbed his face, then looked across at the black-haired young man hissing at him to be quiet.

"It might come back!"

"What?" Wolflock grumbled, squashing snow to his face to numb the pain.

"The fjallarugal."

Wolflock closed his mouth, his wide blue eyes cutting through the soft light for any trace of the creature.

"How do you know it was the fjallarugal?" he asked, crawling to the top of the embankment.

"I heard it scream, then, the next thing I know, something sharp cut the back of my head and took off with my turban."

"You didn't see anything?"

"It's invisible! What was I meant to see?" the olive-skinned man trembled with terror.

Curiosity seized Wolflock, and he got to his feet, making deliberate movements around the clearing to the turban.

"What are you doing?" Tareq whispered.

"Getting your headwear. What does it look like?"

"Leave it! It's fake!"

Wolflock laughed through his nose and eyed the tracks on the ground. The clearest ones were Tareq's footprints above the local wildlife. Deer, small mammals, a few birds with toes as long as his pinkie finger. The unstrung turban weighed into the snow like a sleeping serpent. Wolflock looked from where it had come, expecting to see the giant, dragon-like footprints Sangur had told them about last night, but he could only see shoe prints.

With his left hand, he scooped up the turban and bundled it together. Something looked strange about the footprints. One set had a curled up toe like Parihaan and Haatji's shoes. Another set crossing it had a distinct outline all the way around. Wolflock thought he could even make out a strange geometric pattern. No creature had attacked Tareq. It had been a human.

But why?

Wolflock felt a leaf from above land on his hair and he raised his hand to brush it off in case it held any water or snow. He didn't want to worry about drying wet hair in this kind of cold. The leaf felt dry, though, and strangely soft. He looked at it more carefully and saw it wasn't a leaf at all. It was a feather as long as his hand.

Wolflock looked up, but could only see pure white snow above the branches. A footstep crunched behind him and he whirled about to see Sangur looking at him with wide eyes, crouching with one hand on his sleek boot pocket and a long dagger in hand. For a moment, his gut leapt, and he thought he was right about the guide master. A deafening shriek shook the trees above them and a huge creature splintered the branches as it crashed down towards them.

"RUN!" Sangur shouted.

Wolflock didn't need telling twice. He pelted through the snow and up the hill, following the guide and Tareq, throwing all the strength his legs had left into hauling himself up the hill. The heavy thuds of the steps hitting the ground through the snow shook him as he tumbled up the slope, but he didn't stop or look behind for a moment. He could feel the hot breath on the back of his neck and the savage snap of the monster chasing him. The thunking sound its jaws made urged him on harder.

Just as he saw the other two vanish, and he thought it would snatch him away, he burst through the trees into the clearing and fell into the dirt beside one of the tents. The three of them tried to pant silently, careening their ears to listen, but no sound followed them over the ridge.

"Fjalla... rugal," Sangur wheezed.

"You... saved my life..." Wolflock panted back. "If you... hadn't come... It might have eaten me."

Sangur nodded, his shoulders rising and falling slower as his breathing steadied.

"Why was it here?" Tareq's green eyes stayed as wide as saucers. "I thought it only came at night."

Sangur hoisted himself to his feet and frowned at Wolflock with a stare that was all too familiar to the amateur sleuth.

"Too many people disobeyed the last rule."

Rhiannon D. Elton

CHAPTER 6

The Science & Spirituality
of Knives

on't stare into the darkness. It will stare back."
The eighth rule brought any chatter over dinner to
a whisper and most of the party stared into the fire,
frightened to look away. Wolflock couldn't help but
glance to his side every time he heard a noise in the dark
snowy landscape beyond the flickering light of the fire.
His nerves were on edge, and, when Thuthukta asked
Sangur for a fork instead of a spoon, Wolflock nearly fell
off his seat.

"Do you have family in Shellinden?" the one eyed man asked.

"How did you know?" said the guide with a chuckle.

"This fork. It has a Shellinden makers seal. It's nice."

"Keep it for the trip. I'm more of a spoon person myself."

Wolflock sat with Tareq as far away from the woods as they could in the circle.

The Uluken boy looked no more than a half decade older than Wolflock, and his troubled face fiddled with his turban as he carefully re-affixed it. The sleuth watched in fascination as Tareq smoothed every careful fold back into taut perfection and turned each gold, dangling chain and medallion so they laid flat on the magenta fabric.

As Wolflock looked over his ringed fingers, bangled wrists and long embroidered sleeves, he could see that, like his own clothes, Tareq's were worn from travel. But unlike his own, all of Tareq's were fake. The green tinges along his fingers and the lighter side of his wrist told Wolflock that cheaper metals with gold plating were not just there for show, but had been there for quite some time. His high-collared coat had the most intricate golden thread embroidered along the hems, but had been blended with the yellow thread from which the dye had leaked from the snow, making it damp. He could also smell the distinct pinch of turmeric, especially as they warmed by the fire.

His high collar could be the same as the man with the knife. And I might have seen his turban and not a bald head in the darkness. But he travelled for months with Shĭmìsī. Unless this is the culprit in disguise, he's not the man I'm after.

"Shĭmìsī mentioned you came with her from the Uluken pass." Wolflock said as he finished his dinner.

Tareq's shoulders relaxed as he finished putting his headwear back on. "Yes. This is true."

"Is the entire journey on foot? We travelled by river."

"Who is we?" Tareq's thick black eyebrows drew together. Wolflock caught a glimpse of the regrowth from where he had plucked the hairs out to separate and shape them.

"Myself and..." Wolflock looked to Mothy, who was nodding back to Etienne's medical chatter with bored grey eyes.

"I didn't know that. Incredible," Mothy laughed and scratched his ear.

At least he knows he's smarter than that useless idiot.

"... my friend. We made it just in time on the Silver Ice Hair."

"Ah yes. They're the fastest passenger vessel in the West. Well... the river West. You have to look at the Tamamuki ships for fast coastal travel."

Wolflock raised an eyebrow. He had expected Tareq to be uninformed as well as terrible at business.

"Do you know a lot about the trade routes in Puinteyle?"

Tareq smiled, his green eyes glittering the way some did when someone brought up a topic they were proficient and passionate about. "I certainly do. The history of trading routes and available resources in the different countries was my favourite subject. I've been able to successfully predict the biggest waves in economic growth for the past three years."

Wolflock lowered his voice so as not to embarrass the man. "If that is so, why is your jewellery fake?"

As he expected, Tareq flushed red and stammered. "I-I-I-Who? Why would you-?"

"I'm not going to tell anyone else unless it's hurting them. I'm just curious. You seem knowledgeable. Why would there be reports and evidence of poor business practices with you?"

"Listen," he put a finger up between them, "I had a bad run, but I've turned it around. Or... I'm about to. Glass is going to become a very valuable commodity in the next few years. I'm just ahead of my time, is all. You'll see. They'll all see."

"You were accustomed to being correct about all your predictions for quite some time, weren't you? You have the same tone I hear from myself. Just with less certainty."

"No! It's true. Glass is going to be the next big thing."

Wolflock knew if he pushed on the subject more, he'd exasperate his acquaintance. "What do you know about knives?"

Tareq blinked. "Pardon?"

"Shĭmìsī said you had a very fancy set of knives. I find that the various properties of a blade can be exceedingly useful in my investigations. For instance, I have a particular crime I thought you may be able to assist me with."

Tareq leaned in closer, eyes wide and eager to hear more.

"Shĭmìsī noticed that someone has been stealing food. Now, the easy guess is that it's her, but the damage to the box was in a most peculiar shape. If you were to show me the knife set within your possession, I could not only clear you from any suspicion, but, also, I would be one step closer to finding the thief."

"But what about the knife that killed that man? Could this help you find him too? I would go and get them now, but I..." He looked into the darkness. Wolflock saw the recollection of the eighth rule flash in his eyes and he jerked his head back around to the fire.

"Possibly." Wolflock bit his cheek as he stitched together a lie. If Tareq was the killer, he'd have to make sure he didn't know he was on his trail. "It's a very strange blade, though. I'm sure it looks like a pole with spikes or something. Or a hunting arrow with a razor head."

"I suppose there are a lot of hunters on the mountain around this time of year. If you come with me after dinner, I'll show you."

"Why wait? I have a solution to the dark," Wolflock chuckled, whipping out his grey match and striking it on the log.

"Necromancy? Expensive. Where did you get that?"

"It was a gift from Dr Qwan for helping to clear out an issue with the Creast Bay." Wolflock got to his feet.

"Ah. That is their best festival of the year. It brings

in a lot of business and supplies that they rely on through the Winter. I'm shocked the mayor didn't give you his firstborn." Tareq laughed and pushed himself up off the log he sat on. "Granted, a light like that is worth a pretty deimas."

As Tareq led them to his tent, which he shared with Professor Thuthukta Isisodwa, he mentioned which friends of his practised secret necromancy at the university.

"It's not outlawed, but it's definitely not taught. They're very careful, though. You don't play with dead things if they're not sanitised, and you don't play with magic unless you know the science behind it."

"Do you do any magic?" Wolflock asked as he followed Tareq into his tent, staying by the flap in case he was still potentially dangerous.

"Just the normal kind. I pray every meal to Haje and give her thanks, and, when I groom my nails, I summon focus and open Haje's divine stream of wealth to my hands for me to receive and pass along."

"That sounds like faith. Not magic. I meant spells and sigils. Things like that."

Tareq gave him a patronising smile. "You understand once you start practising. The way you think is everything. Divine magic is powerful. Feast your eyes, my friend."

He drew out a crimson box and lifted the gold hinged lid to reveal an exquisite set of golden knives with jewelled handles. Although they had been polished to a reflective quality, they had deep scars from time.

"These were the ceremonial blades of the son of Sira Wafira, the most esteemed high priestess of Haje's temple. They say she travelled the world and learned about the flow of wealth and fortune in every nation."

It was the most impractical set of knives he'd seen in his entire life. Curves and squiggles, with holes in them. Even one with spikes like a shark jaw.

"Are they genuine gold?"

"Actually, no. They're even better than that. The legend says that Haje reached down from the heavens to bless Sira Wafira, and she cracked the goddess's hand with a golden bolt of lightning, creating these golden stones. There is no flexibility in them whatsoever. They're not to be used in anything except a ritual."

Tareq looked proud of his collection, but Wolflock's face flattened with disappointment. None of them had three blades or a swirl to them at all. One caught his eye, though.

"That looks more like a spatula than a knife."

"This one is the best for cutting Jevastal delight."

Tareq lifted it out as if he were trying to lift a sand sculpture.

Wolflock knew Myna had fond memories of Jevastal delight. It was a sugary rose jelly that could withstand hot temperatures, so it didn't melt in Summer. It was far too sickly sweet for Wolflock's tastes.

The knife, if it could be called that, was a broad triangular shape with jagged edges, flaring out broader than Wolflock's hand and coming back into the handle. It was pretty and antique, and just the right shape and size to have left marks on the food crate.

"How brittle are they?"

"Oh, I wouldn't be using this on anything tougher than a soft cake during a ritual. Even one with nuts in it may be dangerous." Tareq placed the knife back in the case with the same delicacy.

Wolflock leaned forward, holding the match low enough to examine the jagged, stony edges. "How do you clean these?" There wasn't a trace of wood, blood, or sticky sweet Jevastal delight.

"Oh, I never!" Tareq gasped. "Anything, even water, might corrode the blades. I give them a very light dusting with a peacock's feather once a month. Nothing more, nothing less."

A frown creased Wolflock's face. "Do you know if

Thuthukta would know anything about them?"

Tareq's face darkened. "I don't think the professor would know much. He hasn't spoken a word to me except to give instructions about the way we should put up the tent. It's the other teacher who would be capable of that."

"Ms Pakuna?" Wolflock scoffed. He highly doubted the nervous woman could be much of a threat to anyone.

"Yes. Her. She had a go at me out of nowhere, when I wanted to show her my assignment. Just as a talking point, you know? She flew into a rage at me, but not before I saw her notes. She's building something. I could see it."

Wolflock had seen it too, but it hadn't looked sinister as Tareq's tone would suggest.

"She would probably be able to tell you how she made the strange pole knife you're asking about. Just don't ask her about her notes. Otherwise, you'll lose favour, too."

Wolflock snorted. "I try not to care about favour much, anyway. I hadn't considered that it would be a hard device to make, though."

"Maybe not with glass. But making anything with metal is too difficult, as far as I'm concerned."

"I'll have a talk with her. In the meantime, perhaps don't tell anyone else you've passed your assignment while you were away. Webs of lies get very tangled when other people know the truth."

Tareq opened his mouth to protest, then closed it and slumped in defeat.

"It's hard, you know? I'm the golden child in the business department at the university. I'm meant to be perfect. Never to make mistakes. They rely on me to show them the way."

Wolflock raised an eyebrow. He didn't want to upset Tareq, but he couldn't oblige lies from a fellow intellectual. What would Mothy say?

"Well... You may be giving them a far more important demonstration by being honest. By showing them your mistakes, you make them understand the reality of your studies and they can watch out for the same pitfalls. The collective knowledge comes from mistakes." Wolflock offered him his hand to help him out of the tent. "Trust me. This is coming from someone who was never considered the golden child. I'm the black sheep. The one everyone relies on to ruin family gatherings and public festivals."

"You don't seem that bad," Tareq chuckled.

"Oh, you haven't seen anything yet. Wait until I get

a proper thread for the food thief and the murderer. Mothy says I'm quite stubborn. I say I'm determined."

"Are you sure he's your friend? He seems to be in a lot of pain."

Wolflock didn't answer. He still didn't understand what he could have done that was so wrong in Mothy's eyes.

"I'm hoping it's just nerves about being so close to our destination."

They made their way back to the fire where Blayne entertained the circle with his own poetry.

"... And although he lay friendless, once my foe, now my fellow, I rest the pieces of my heart before the vow to pretend less."

The group clapped, but Wolflock sensed they didn't quite know what for. Tareq clapped loudly and took his seat next to Etienne. The only other person to clap quite so emphatically was Drua, who had overcome her bout of anger. Wolflock sat beside Ms Pakuna and warmed his hands on the fire in front of him. He brewed a cup of wild lettuce tea and sipped it to calm his nerves before questioning the teacher. The anxious teacher kept her hands latched to her knees, shivering.

"Are you cold, ma'am?" he asked.

"What? Oh. No. Not at all. The fire is hot."

"But are you cold? You're shivering?"

She shook her head and continued to tremble.

He caught Mothy's eye on the other side of her. For a moment it was that curious blue Wolflock thought was his natural eye colour, but it sunk into a hazel as he realised they were still at odds.

"What are you going to teach at the university, Ms Pakuna?" Mothy asked as he received a second serve of dinner.

"Huh? Oh, me? I-I'm teaching engineer-eering. Mmhmm." She nodded rapidly.

Wolflock blinked. She said she wasn't cold and he didn't note nervousness in her tone, even with her stutter. "An engineer? What kind?"

"M-metal tr-transport a-a-and applianc-ces. A-are y-you both st-studying engineering?" She twitched her head to the side and brought it back to normal just as quickly.

Wolflock and Mothy made eye contact again and realised they both understood why she was shivering. Ms Pakuna had a nervous condition that made her tremble and twitch. Wolflock had seen this before in his favourite music tutor. While he prepared the music lessons, his hands shook and his voice quaked, but, the moment he played any instrument or sang, they melted away.

"That is so fascinating. We're not studying engineering, but I do have a puzzle you may be able to help me with." Wolflock took out his journal and flicked to his sketch of the swirling three bladed knife. "How would someone go about making this?"

"M-may I?" She held out a shaking hand for his pencil and journal.

Wolflock nodded and handed her the book, ready to snatch it back in case she did anything.

Ms Pakuna put the pencil to a blank page and started writing with her right hand. "The only time I've seen a knife like this is from Chalongesh." She spoke without a stutter and her body relaxed. "I'm an engineer, so I prefer rigid parts and things that don't squish the same as a body. Wood, metal and fabric are my elements. This weapon, though, I know it. In South Pyringel, they still have to deal with weapons like this from the barbarian houses that cross the border. They think the land is theirs. This weapon isn't just made to kill. It's made to maim. If you use this to stab fabric or rubber, you would not be able to fix it without a patch. If you stabbed a human with this, you would not be able to stitch the wound. You'd have to cauterise it."

Wolflock looked up at Mothy as Ms Pakuna started sketching something in the back of his journal to keep away her twitches. His friend had paled at the mention of his home country. He realised that Mothy had started disadvantaged, but, no matter where he went in Chalongesh, he would have come in contact with terrible violence.

"Why are you a Ms and not a professor? And why Mystentine? Pyringel has a university too, doesn't it?" Wolflock asked.

She hummed a native Pyringel Lullaby as she flicked over the page and scratched out a sketch of a two wheeled device with a rigid sail on top of it. "It's my first year at the university. After I complete my tutorage, I'll be a professor. As for your second question, Mystentine has a better engineering program. The social studies and biology studies are greater in Pyringel. They saw me create this," she showed them the vehicle sketch, "and knew I would be a good fit."

"What is that? It looks like fun." Mothy asked, dog earring the page.

"It is!" Ms Pakuna laughed, continuing to make little sketches on her original page. "I built it because, in Pyringel, we ride the winds. Ta'akin Point City is built onto the cliffs and we used gliders to soar up and down. Hunters use them over the plains. But, when someone becomes injured or their bodies deteriorate, they can't fly anymore. I saw my grandparents waste away through the sadness of not being able to ride the winds. So I took a Chalongesh's friend's two wheeled design and put a sail on it. Now the people don't need to fear age to fly."

Wolflock smiled at the genius of the device.

"The other engineering staff at Mystentine want to help design it and make light flight travel widespread. I am so excited to be part of this. The joy of flying is only known to birds, witches and us in Pyringel. It's such a blessing to share it with the world."

"And dragons," Wolflock added.

"Oh yes! Of course. And dragons. There aren't many in Pyringel."

"And the knife? How would that be made?" he persisted.

"I... I'm not sure. A special anvil or welding it through the centre and then turning it. It could also be from a mould."

"With three sharp edges, I can't imagine it's easy to sheath," Wolflock muttered.

"Definitely not. I can't see a leather pouch holding this. Even a hardened one. Metal would blunt it. It would have to be stored in a wooden cylinder of some kind. Or metal with fabric lining."

Wolflock frowned, looking around the group.

"You don't seriously think it's someone here?" Mothy snapped.

Wolflock flashed a look back at his glaring friend and maintained a stony expression. "Would anyone use that for hunting?"

Ms Pakuna shook her head, closing the journal and returning it back to Wolflock's hands with his pencil. "No. This weapon is used to maim. It is not kind like a hunter's quick kill. If you th-think it is s-someone here, I c-c-cannot help you. I won't-t r-risk my career for g-gossip. S-sorry."

With a polite nod, she rose and made her way to her tent, but not before giving Professor Thuthukta a nervous squeak as she bumped into him. Wolflock's head snapped around as he heard the dull thunk of her hitting the cylinder of bamboo he had kept at his hip all this time.

Rhiannon D. Elton

CHAPTER 7

Worst Friend, Meet Best Friend

The wind howled, dimming the fire and any remaining desire to stay out in the darkness. Sangur ordered everyone to head to bed and not leave their tents until dawn.

"Remember rules five and eight. Shelter, water, food, in that order, and don't look into the darkness. Unless it's the back of your eyelids."

Most of the party scurried off to bed as snow fell across them. Wolflock noticed that Thuthukta walked to his tent with a slow confidence. Was it because he knew he was the most dangerous thing out here? Because Wolflock had seen Yifi transform with an enchanted necklace, he couldn't rule out Thuthukta being Astraxis in disguise. His taciturn nature, lack of speaking to anyone, and the cylindrical bamboo container in which he could hide the swirling knife, were all clues directing Wolflock's web to him.

He crawled into his tent alongside Blayne and, in the darkness, he pretended to take off his shoes and laid down. Blayne prattled on about the poems he'd read on their last night and how he planned to look Drua right in the eye and have her heart in his hand.

"I hope Sangur plays his guitar tomorrow so I can sing with him.Only with false modesty, do I say I can't sing like a nightingale."

"I heard he is very good. Be careful or he'll outshine you," Wolflock muttered.

Blayne went very quiet after that and, eventually, Wolflock heard his breathing deepen and slow. When he was satisfied the camp had fallen asleep, he rolled forward and slipped out of the tent. He let his eyes adjust to the darkness. The moon was barely a slither of white in the sky, but the swirls of misty stars gave him enough light to make out the tents, ropes and trees against the dark white snow. Wolflock trod across the soft ground, feeling like every crunch was a thunder roll.

Soon, Wolflock reached Tareq and Thuthukta's tent and slowly pulled back the rear flap. He couldn't see Thuthukta. He and his cylinder had disappeared.

Wolflock growled in frustration and stood up straight. Where could he have gone? He had listened so carefully. He struck his match up and saw footprints leading away from the tent. A clean print with a deep square tread. That may have been the geometric pattern he saw earlier, but he hadn't seen it well enough. Perhaps his luggage on the wagon would yield better results.

He made his way along the least snowy path to the wagon, where the goats baa-ed softly, the same way they did when Fiddi or Urgi pet them. Wolflock gave Dergi's neck a wobble and moved to the back of the wagon, where it was easier to get onto it.

As he rounded the corner, he felt a hand wrap around his shoulder and haul him back. Wolflock flailed and made an indent in the snow. The match went out and Wolflock grabbed clumps of snow until he found it a few moments later. The figure didn't move any closer as he struck it on the side of the wagon.

Wolflock squinted as the light flared up again. "Mothy?" He let out a sigh of relief. "Thank goodness.

Listen, I'm on a fantastic trail. I found a thread. There is evidence that Astraxis didn't just find us, but he's here. He's somewhere in the company. He killed that man in the cave and I am so close to finding the answer. You can't say that doesn't sound like fun, right? I saw how you jumped in with Ms Pakuna earlier. You're so much more useful than Blayne."

The blond boy clenched his fists by his sides and stared down at Wolflock with eyes black with contempt and fury. Not quite the response he expected. He got to his feet and brushed off the snow from his jacket.

"This is all your fault."

"What?"

Mothy grabbed the front of his coat and shook him, then pointed at the ground behind the wagon. Giant, three-toed, bird-like footprints imprinted the snow.

"If, and I say IF, Astraxis is here, then he followed you because you're too stupid to keep your nose out of where it doesn't belong. You're the reason the fjallarugal is following us. And you're the reason I have to talk to a moron every-"

Wolflock's face remained blank through Mothy's rant until he said the word 'moron', and his eyebrow rose.

"You need to stop," Mothy said as he collected himself, letting go of Wolflock's jacket. "You're putting everyone in danger and you don't care. You'll destroy innocent and vulnerable people to get your answers."

"Mothy, I do nothing but care. I care that the man at the centre of a mind controlling, alcohol smuggling, gambling, slavery ring is at large and in close proximity to us, threatening our lives and the people we with travel with. How is that my fault?" Wolflock snarled, rage boiling in his veins.

"You have a sick sense of justice and think you're the bloody god of intellect! For once in your life, just follow the rules!"

"The rules never mattered when we were on the same team, Mothy! You're a stupid fool for not helping me!"

"What is stupidity but vanity and naivety?" drawled Blayne as he circled around the goats and tied his luxurious quilted blue dressing gown.

Both Mothy and Wolflock rounded on Blayne and glared. Wolflock sneered and hoisted himself onto the wagon.

"What are you doing here? This isn't any of your business," Mothy hissed.

Wolflock had never heard anything like it come from Mothy's mouth.

"Your eyes are so peculiar. How did you get black

with that green slice? Is that why this one fascinated you, Felen?"

Mothy's nose wrinkled in disgust, but Wolflock started digging through the boxes and trunks, using their argument for cover.

"It's just like him to find another arrogant, self-entitled rich boy. You two are a perfect match."

Ignoring what Mothy thought were insults and what Blayne thought were compliments, Wolflock unlatched three trunks and a chest, finding nothing but clothes, dried foods, and books.

"At least he has deimas to rub together. Not as much as me, clearly, but you should stop your mooching."

"Mooching? Mooching! No amount of money can buy class or manner."

In one of the crates from the two men who didn't have prior permission to load cargo, Wolflock found a ledger. Signatures from Lord Therym were all over it. Tucked into it were letters from Therym to Astraxis. His hands chilled.

This was Astraxis's box.

He dug deeper. Musical paper with letters from Najord, and receipts from the Twin Pines lumber mill for storage, which left two weeks before they arrived. What was more alarming, though, were the letters from Volseggir and Chestir asking for further instructions with paper stamped with the Xed eye.

Wolflock had completely tuned out Mothy and Blayne arguing. The collection of letters, the ledger and the symbols were a perfect box of evidence. As if it were all ready to be bundled up just for him. It was perfect.

Too perfect.

Wolflock's lips twisted in disgust. Astraxis had done this before. He planted evidence on Parihaan and his flunky Najord had done the same with his own father. It made him wonder if there were even more instances where Astraxis had shown a glimpse of his hand to divert Wolflock's attention away.

Wolflock dug just a little deeper and found a letter addressed to Amery Blayne's father, stamped with the Xed eye. Wolflock's thumb pressed into the ink and he laughed as it smeared. Astraxis was trying to frame Blayne.

With a smirk, he opened the largest box. There had to be unplanned clues here somewhere, and he was going to find them.

It was empty.

He frowned. Why cart an empty box? Except... it wasn't empty when the men had put it on the wagon.

Astraxis had been in the box until the first evening when Wolflock had seen him by the wagon. That meant he knew where and when they were going up the mountain. He'd gotten that information... from Chestir? Captain Estivan and Officer Tand? How?

Wolflock closed the lid of the chest and tried to open the last one. It was a box three times the size of a shoebox and was the only locked one. The lock was new, but the latch was old and the nails holding it into the wood looked loose. Wolflock drew out his penknife and wedged it under the latch. With a sharp push, it broke free.

Herbs.

Eight compartments with different herbs. Dried purple flowers; flakes of purple sea slug; dried black berries with pointy purple flowers; long stems with orange, bell-shaped flowers; three compartments filled with different dried green leaves; and a last one had a familiar, dried stem, barely as thick as twine.

"Mothy. I have herbs up here. I require your identification skills."

The arguing boys stopped and Mothy glared at Wolflock up on the wagon. He pushed the box closer to the edge and Mothy looked closer. Wolflock did everything he could to not smile. He held the match closer to help Mothy see the plants.

"Some kind of Datura, dried meat, deadly nightshade, wolfsbane, coca leaves, oleander leaves, some kind of dried cactus, and... ephedra? Wolflock, is this yours?"

He shook his head. "Why do you ask?"

"Poisons and the kind of stimulants that would keep you awake indefinitely? How did you get this?"

"I'm not sure what to say. I'm flattered you think I know anything about herbs? I've just seen this one before." He pinched up the ephedra. The little, twig-like stems crunched under his fingers.

He felt something touch the top of his head. He thought he heard one of the goats make a strange cooing snore. Putting his hand on his head, he found a soft leaf. But they weren't under any trees. Wolflock looked up but only saw the black sky. No stars or anything. He looked at his leaf and saw it.

A white feather.

"I'm sure you have. It's how you bother everyone at all hours of the evening."

"What are you lot doing?" Sangur's voice boomed through the campsite. "Get off the wagon-"

As Sangur ran towards them, a wave of pounding wind blasted Wolflock off the wagon, followed by an ear-piercing scream. Against the black sky, Wolflock looked up and only just made out a vague, round shape standing on top of the goats. The trunks and crates from the top of the wagon crashed to the ground as the fjallarugal scrambled over the top of it towards the boys.

"Get under the wagon!" Sangur shouted, but Wolflock had already gotten to his feet and ran around the outside of the clearing, away from the monster.

Mothy and Blayne squatted under the wagon, but Wolflock's run distracted the beast. He heard its snapping jaws and rumbling feet chase him, crashing into the trees and shattering branches as it gained on him. His only thought was that he had to lead it away. He couldn't go for cover in his tent. It would crush the other campers. He had one choice. He circled around to the path that led down to where it had chased him up from.

He felt its hot screaming breathing over his shoulder and leaped over the crest of the hill, sloping down to the clearing he'd found Tareq in. Just in time, he caught a tree root and laid flat in the grass. A thunderous whoosh soared over him and the trees all the way down to the clearing cracked and snapped as the fjallarugal chased an invisible Wolflock back down the mountain.

He rested back in the soothing cold snow for a moment and let out the breath he'd been holding.

Worried it might come back, Wolflock ran back to scramble into his tent and found Blayne curled up in the foetal position.

"You're alive!" he gasped.

Wolflock chuckled and took his shoes off before getting into dry clothes. "I have been up against sea storms, vampiric horses and very desperate people. An invisible mountain monster isn't enough to end me."

Blayne laughed nervously back, but, for once, didn't respond.

The adrenaline coursing through his veins crashed, leaving Wolflock tired and achy in the late hours of the evening. He kept a keen ear out for the return of the fjallarugal as he drifted off into a light sleep, thinking of the box of medicines.

Doctors use medicine... and some doctors use medicine poorly. He frowned as he dreamed of his mental web tying its threads to Etienne. Was Mothy in even worse danger? Had Astraxis, under the disguise of Etienne, caused a wedge between them as well as lured his best friend away?

Rhiannon D. Elton

CHAPTER 8

The Toolless & Witless

Wolflock's eyes felt bleary as he woke late the next morning. Blayne had slept in as well. Birds chirped and people chatted outside in hushed whispers. His body ached from the walking, the running and the fearing for his life. Today was their last full day of travel and he had to solve the case before evening, otherwise, the fjallarugal would get to them again.

He groaned and stretched as he pulled on his travelling clothes, not sure if he could run the same way he did last night. Crawling out of the tent, he saw Shĭmìsī had prepared a mountain of pancakes and thin, crispy slices of sweet potato.

"Good morning." Wolflock rubbed his eyes as he sat by the tired-looking chef. The bags under her eyes told him she had slept poorly as well.

"Good morning."

"You slept as well as I did, I see."

She gave him a coy smile. "Was that you chasing off the food thief last night?"

Wolflock laughed. "No, that was me getting chased by the fjallarugal. Maybe it thought I was the food thief."

"Did Tareq have the knife you were looking for?"

"No. His aren't useful. Brittle,antique things. One of them is in the right shape to have caused the damage on the box, but it's not strong enough."

"I hope you have more ideas about who is stealing the food. We only have enough left for lunch and, if anymore goes missing, we're going to arrive at the university starving."

Wolflock pressed his lips together in a flat line. While on a case he'd forget to eat often, but he knew Mothy wouldn't survive without three meals. He was always hungry.

"Do you think we can forage for something on the way?"

Shĭmìsī shook her head. "No. I do not know these

lands and it's snowing. Maybe Sangur knows better. I hope Urgi joins us with more food."

The company packed up their tents and cooking materials, and set off again up the ever-increasing slope. The road twisted through patches of trees and around enormous boulders so tall that the snow couldn't blanket them, but rather, gave them skirts and hats. Eventually, the company stepped in line behind the giant goats as they cut a trench through the snow.

Sangur sat on the wagon with Fiddi, looking over the map from his compass. Wolflock thought it was odd that he would need to look over the map in the first place, but it could have been from all the snowfall changing the appearance of the landmarks the guide relied on. His focus was more on the medical students and their possible connection to the herbs.

Etienne and Mothy were locked in conversation with the excited Drua, who kept looking back at Blayne as he sang his poems into the icy air. An idea struck Wolflock.

"What do you know about the Merris', Blayne?"

Blayne stopped singing, which made a few of the others sigh with relief. It wasn't that he was a terrible singer. He was quite melodic. It's just that he sang the same song over and over, saying he would get it perfect, eventually.

"He's a perfect gentleman. Very learned. What are

you prying for?" Blayne drawled, as if he had a menu for Wolflock to choose from.

Wolflock gave him a contemptuous smirk. "He has information that may make us fast friends. Or enemies. Depending on his answers."

Blayne nodded. "Ah. Yes. I'm with you. I'm surprised it took you this long to figure it out."

Wolflock raised an eyebrow, but Blayne didn't notice. What had this dolt known that he didn't? How could he have found out about the medicines before Wolflock did?

"You definitely haven't ingratiated yourself to him, though. Poking and prodding and embarrassing him and his sister. What are you prepared to do to garner the favour of the one who stole your servant?"

"Would hitting you help?" Wolflock sneered; hearing the word 'servant' again flared his anger.

"Definitely not. For starters, I was the thrice wrestling champion of my school and you look like a rake. And, secondly, the one you want information from is a fond acquaintance of mine, and threats are not going to get you closer to what you seek." Blayne waggled his finger with a smug grin.

Wolflock rolled his eyes. "And why do I need to do anything to appease the useless medical student? I don't owe him anything, and he certainly hasn't earned my respect."

Blayne gasped, but he couldn't hide his snide smile. "My word, Mr Felen. Either your family was improperly wealthy, and you had no reason to abide by societal structures, or you have the arrogance of a lion. Either way, this is going to be enormously entertaining."

Blayne linked arms with Wolflock and dragged him forward to the chatting group, skipping over a snow mound. "Oh, Mr Merris," he sang and shoved Mothy away to make space between Etienne and Drua. "I have a very curious cat here who may need some medical advice."

"Oh? Sedation or elevation?" Etienne sneered.

Wolflock scoffed. "Not for me. I was after information on something specific, like ephedra or wolfsbane."

"Ah. Those... umm... You probably shouldn't be trying to make witches' potions during our travels. If you need to sleep, just eat more for dinner and it'll knock you right out. Shame we don't have any milk."

Wolflock frowned, glancing at Mothy, whose nose wrinkled as the medical student spoke. Seeing Etienne was confused, he turned to his sister. "Ah. You know about it, don't you, Drua? You seem like you've been studying medicine well."

Drua flushed as Wolflock addressed her. She took the insincerity of his compliment and pouted. "Of course I know, but I shan't say a word. Sleeping herbs are dangerous in unskilled hands."

"So you didn't bring any with you?" Wolflock exhaled through his nose, wondering if they brought the herbs and have been using them incorrectly or if they hadn't brought them at all.

"Oh, stars and moon, no!" Drua gasped in the exact same way Blayne did, just without the sarcasm.

"And dandelion, then?" Wolflock huffed, glancing at Mothy.

Etienne scoffed. "Who uses weeds like that these days? Manufacturing the tinctures and extracts is far more potent for any physician."

Mothy's face fell, and he backed away. Then, as Drua backed her brother up about his pharmaceutical prowess, he sped up and sat on the wagon, pretending to check the ropes.

"So one of the most useful and potent liver tonics is not something you're interested in?" Wolflock scoffed loud enough for Mothy to hear.

"And what would you know?" Drua snapped. "Didn't you hear him? Extracts and tonics are far superior to-"

"How do you extract medicine from herbs?"

The siblings both closed their mouths and Blayne grinned.

"Well... you... you distil it into medical alcohol." Etienne spoke slowly.

"Have you ever seen a person suffering from liver problems? Because Mothy and I have. You can't put alcohol anywhere near them. It can be lethal."

"S-so can be ephedra!" Etienne stammered, trying to catch up where he had lost face. "It's terrible on the liver. I remember now. Yes. Yes, that's right. You keep it away from people with jaundice. Far away."

Wolflock blinked. He had seen ephedra stems around Parihaan before she fell down the stairs. Astraxis had tried to kill her on the ship and make it look like liver failure.

"You have to give it up, Felen. You're just not a physician, and Mr Merris here is well on his way to being the grandest doctor in all of Puinteyle."

Etienne's shoulders shrugged with relief. "Thank you, Amery."

"And don't fret yourself, friend. Felen may be out to destroy your career, but, with my influence, he won't have any credit amongst your peers."

Drua's face split into a nasty grin. "You're so

charming, Amery. Even this fool couldn't withstand your skills of persuasion."

Wolflock raised an eyebrow and stopped walking. Blayne and Merris hadn't known each other until they came to Mystentine. Because of the delays ascending the mountain, they had likely stayed at the same lodgings nearby as they waited. Blayne had no issue talking with the pretender, but there was something else here. Blayne had boasted so much about his wealth and contacts. Merris was failing his degree and couldn't recall basic medical details and pharmacology. He certainly couldn't perform any physical therapy safely; Wolflock's ankle was proof of that. But they each had something to gain.

Merris could use Blayne's supposed connections to keep himself from failing, unleashing a dangerous doctor onto the continent, but what could Merris offer Blayne?

Something Blayne had said before the conversation with Merris had started. Something that Wolflock hadn't figured out about Merris. Something that he could offer wealthy and prestigious folk, as Blayne assumed Wolflock was. His eyes narrowed as he watched the self-important trio strutting away from him. If he was able to go through Merris's things, he felt sure he'd find medications he wasn't qualified to give out that Blayne had an interest in.

He started to concoct a plan to do just that when a

box and a trunk crashed off the wagon. The box of herbs splintered over the hard ground, and the trunk burst open, filled with white lab coats and grooming products. Wolflock's eyes shot up to Mothy, sitting on the back of the wagon. His angry, dark eyes stared right at Merris.

"My case!" Merris shouted and ran forward.

Sangur and Fiddi stopped the goats in response to the commotion and the company watched on.

"Whoops." Mothy shrugged, hopping off the wagon and stretching. "I must have been leaning on the wrong rope. Sorry."

He didn't sound sorry. He also didn't move to help. He lazily stepped over the mess and walked around the wagon and spoke to Shǐmìsī.

Wolflock jogged up to the mess to pretend to help by catching the papers blowing away. He saw that Merris had paid no heed to the herb box. Only his clothes and toiletries.

The box isn't his. Those aren't his herbs. Wolflock looked at Blayne and Miss Merris, as they snickered. They aren't upset about the herb box either.

"Help me, damnit!" Merris snapped at them. His sister dropped down and immediately obeyed, but Blayne caught Wolflock's eye with an evil sneer.

He dug his hands into the wagon and heaved with all

his might until he ripped out Mothy's bag. Wolflock's gut twisted.

"Hey! Put that down!" Wolflock shouted.

"Justice is justice," he laughed as he pulled the drawstring top loose. "Your servant didn't take better care of my doctor's bags, so he'd best get to cleaning."

Blayne shook Mothy's bag upside down and let everything fall out. Mothy turned to see it all too late. He ran forward and dived along the cold, hard ground to catch something delicate.

"It was an accident, Amery," Merris said. "No need to be like that."

Blayne shrugged and threw the bag to the ground. "Whoops."

He kicked Mothy's things out of the way as he made his way around the side of the wagon.

"Oh, I don't think so." Wolflock leaped forward and seized him by the shirt.

"Ah. Felen. Showing a bit of backbone now? Good to see," the cruel blond boy laughed in his face.

Wolflock's face contorted with rage, and he shoved Blayne against the side of the wagon. "Help him pick up his things."

"Or what?"

Wolflock drew back his fist to threaten Blayne, but,

before he could do anything, what felt like a rock bashed into his nose. Blayne head-butted him and went to throw a fist into his gut, but two, iron hands grabbed them by the shoulders and held them apart.

"Enough," Professor Thuthukta's voice rumbled like thunder.

Wolflock's eyes came back into focus and his nose burned.

"What happened?" Sangur shouted and gripped his fur hat, dismayed at the sight of the mess behind the wagon. "We don't have time for this! What have you broken?" He growled and paced back and forth, going red in his face under his silky beard. "Clean this up. You'll meet us at the lunch stop. Wolflock, you're responsible for every last leaf from that container." He pressed the heel of his palm on his forehead through his hat. "Actually, Merris, you do it. You're the medical student, so you should know what it all looks like. Carry your own things back and meet us at the lunch stop an hour away."

Sangur looked like he was about to strangle someone as he made his way back to the front of the carriage. "Everyone else, keep walking."

Professor Thuthukta folded his mighty arms and looked down at them with his one eye. The Merris siblings complained about every item they put away, but Wolflock didn't dare speak to the lecturer. The bamboo cylinder hung on Professor Thuthukta's hip, and he laid his hand on it whenever Drua complained about the injustice of the situation. The massive, obsidian man didn't say another word.

Wolflock helped Mothy cram things back into his huge bag. "Do you need me to carry anything? It's a fair way," he whispered.

Mothy looked up at him with a pinched expression. He shook his head and kept packing. Wolflock watched him tuck away his hand carved wooden statues with opal eyes in a side pocket, then stuff clothing around them to hold them in tighter. Wolflock knew Mothy only gave them to the people he treasured. Was he tucking them into the side pocket to stop them from falling out again, or did he still have plans to give them to Merris? Wolflock's stomach churned at the thought.

"This isn't mine," Mothy huffed and flicked a letter at Wolflock.

He started to say that it wasn't his either until he read it.

To whomst it might worry,

Mr Etin Merris is a wonderful student. He has come

to the aid of so many people. Ne'er has there been a more proficient doctor cross my surgery. He has outdoine himself and I am ever thankful for his ultimate wisdom and give my highest recommendation for the amendament of his grade. I look forward to hearing that all wrongs have been writed and for Mr Mers to be able to work in my clinic.

Dr Thrumpis

Wolflock let out a laugh and then stifled it. Merris had received one of the most embarrassing recommendations he'd ever seen. The spelling mistakes, the grammatical errors, and the misspelling of his name made Wolflock think that this doctor had not been in his right mind while transcribing the letter. So he was failing, and, apparently, he was so bad at his profession that he had to find a possibly intoxicated doctor to aid him. The shaking script, dissolved areas of paper, and the odour of the paper reinforced his deductions. He folded it into his pocket and continued helping Mothy pack.

He scanned the ground for more items. Tangled in a pair of socks, Wolflock found one of Mothy's straw dolls. He knew he liked to make them, and that there was a particular one that may have been a representation of his mother, but this wasn't like those. The reeds and grass to make it were newer, and he'd smothered the top of the head in ash to give it the appearance of black hair. Wolflock turned it this way and that before he realised who it was meant to be.

Mothy's eyes went wide when he saw Wolflock holding it and he snatched it away, shoving it into his bag with a savagery that made the dark-haired boy flinch.

"Was that a doll?" Drua jeered.

"Drua, stop. Blayne was rude enough. You don't have to be cruel to impress him. He's not here." Merris snapped his case closed.

Miss Merris tensed and looked away.

"I'm terribly sorry for Mr Blayne's conduct. That was entirely uncalled for."

Wolflock looked at Mothy, both acknowledging together that Merris was only apologising, so he didn't have to pick up the herbs alone.

"Apology accepted. I'm sure it was just a misunderstanding." Mothy nodded and accepted Merris's hand up. They did not offer the same hand to Wolflock.

"Now... about these herbs. What a mess."

"You know all these herbs grow fresh on the mountain here." Wolflock picked up a pinch of the purple dried slug. He wasn't going to let Astraxis have his stores returned in any capacity. "Mothy said earlier that the old, dried ingredients were less potent than fresh, anyway."

"Of course! That must have been the mountain aid kit." Merris laughed. "It would all have to be on the mountain, anyway. Perfect. Mothy, would you kindly assist me in replenishing it so Sangur doesn't get upset? I don't want to play in the dirt here for such a fruitless endeavour."

Mothy sighed and looked around. Wolflock could see him picking random plants and trees that looked convincing. "Sure. Have you got a pair of scissors or a knife?"

Wolflock watched as Etienne felt around his person and shook his head. "No. Sorry."

"Here." Drua plucked out a pair of thread trimming scissors and followed her brother and Mothy along the path.

Wolflock let them get a head start away from him and started collecting pocketfuls of the ingredients, and then buried the rest. As he buried them, his hand stuck to a small ball. One of Lija's sticky pink lollies clung to his pinkie finger. He frowned at it. It was one of the ones coated in a brown sugar that they'd found outside the warehouse where Lija had been abducted.

One of the lollies Wolflock had told Mothy to eat.

His gut plummeted, and his wide blue eyes swept

over the path and trees. No one was anywhere to be seen. He shook as he gripped the lolly in his fist. His heart burned, and he cursed his own stupidity.

The lolly was why he'd lost his best friend, and he didn't know if he'd ever be able to earn his trust again.

CHAPTER 9
The Soft Dark

A low blanket of clouds hid the peak of the mountain from sight, and another layer shrouded Mystentine city. Wolflock couldn't tell if they were at the front or back of the mountain as he caught up to the group setting up for lunch on a rocky outcrop.

"What picturesque views of the grey. Oh, and look. More grey." Blayne laughed as he waved his hands over the foggy land. "Exactly what I paid for."

Wolflock rolled his eyes and looked over the group. Fiddi stayed by the goats and watched them drop over the cliff side, just to climb back up as if they taunted gravity itself. The goats looked cleaner. Their fur shone in the grey light and they didn't scratch or rub on the boulders to relieve their itchiness.

Fiddi must be brushing them regularly. I haven't seen her do it, though. Perhaps it's when no one is watching.

Ms Pakuna sketched in her journal as she spoke at Professor Thuthukta, but her tense face and shaking hand told Wolflock that she was still nervous from the fjallarugal disturbance from last night. Thuthukta sat in silence, staring into the fire with a large tooth shaped in amber hanging around his neck. It looked a lot like Yifi's pendant that allowed her to change her appearance and protect herself from the beauty curse her mother had placed on her.

Tareq sat with a blanket wrapped around his shoulders, looking like a forlorn squat mushroom. Mothy, Etienne and Drua stood in a circle by the cooking fire like old friends, rubbing their arms to keep warm. He didn't feel as if he could approach him on this in front of anyone else.

Wolflock couldn't see Shǐmìsī, though.

"Psst. Wolflock," her voice whispered from behind the wagon.

He moved over to her and looked around to see if

anyone had seen him return. He wondered, for a second, what she could want him for, but her look of pale fear told him everything.

"We're out of food, aren't we?"

She nodded, twisting her fingers.

"There's nothing left? Nothing at all? Have you told Sangur?"

She shook her head. "I... I was frightened he'd yell at me. I haven't been eating any more than anyone else. We would have had a month's worth of food for each of us, but the crates were emptied last night. I'm afraid that, if we don't have food, we won't have the qi to stay warm and climb the mountain."

"And we'll all freeze to death and have our bodies dug out next Spring." Wolflock pinched his chin as he thought. "Listen, don't ask why, but Mothy has had to travel a lot during his life, and much of that was with minimal resources. He may have ways to help. Speak to him privately, though."

"That sounds wonderful," Shǐmìsī clapped. "Will you introduce us?"

Wolflock made a face. "We... aren't on the best terms at present. Having me with you won't build a strong rapport with him."

"I see... What will?"

"Ask him about dandelions. He normally has some on his person."

Shĭmìsī gave Wolflock a warm, squishy hug before tippy tapping over to Mothy and the campfire. He looked over the knots holding the ropes down on the wagon and noticed that they were quite poor. From the look on Mothy's face, he knew his old friend had kicked off Etienne's trunk and the case of herbs on purpose. Likely because he wanted to be rid of the dangerous plants and also to see if they were Etienne's.

Clever. Not subtle though, as Blayne figured him out. But why would an experienced traveller like Sangur tie such poor knots? He's not getting Fiddi to do it for him, is he? She seems competent enough to know how to fasten the cargo down, though. Perhaps it's stress, or Urgi may normally be the one to take care of it.

He didn't have long to think about it as he saw a chain of whispers run through the company. Shĭmìsī spoke to Mothy, Mothy spoke to Ms Pakuna, Ms Pakuna spoke to Professor Thuthukta, and he spoke to Sangur.

Sangur's grey eyes went wide, and he rubbed his forehead through his fur hat. Sangur and Thuthukta spoke back and forth in Shell. Wolflock walked closer to be sure. A Shiriling man and a Syongdelen man speaking Shell was strange separately, but the fact that they spoke it together struck Wolflock as quite odd. What were they trying to hide from the rest of the party?

He looked to Mothy, Blayne and Etienne to see if they had any expressions of understanding. Blayne's eyes widened, and he looked as if the two older men had insulted his vulnerable being. Etienne seemed blank faced and Mothy nodded to himself.

Whatever they're proposing to do, Mothy thinks it's a good idea. At least a reasonable one. Blayne thinks it's a personal insult. It must be labour.

Sangur rose to his feet and clapped his hands to get everyone's attention. "It has come to my attention that we have left one of our supply cases with Urgi at the base of the mountain and we've nearly run out of rations."

The group fell into a tense silence as they listened.

"To alleviate this matter, Professor Thuthukta and I are going to go on a hunting expedition. I encourage the rest of you to continue on the path to our evening campsite and keep a close eye for chanterelle mushrooms, abandoned bird nests, late season berries and... what else?" He leaned down to Ms Pakuna, who looked to Mothy.

"Rose hip berries and dandelions. The roots will be good for a stew. We can also eat the pine nuts, needles and bark as long as it isn't a yew tree and lichen hiding amongst the rocks." Mothy didn't look up as he spoke, but Shĭmìsī gave him an encouraging squeeze around the shoulders to help him speak up.

"There. See? No one is going to starve. Just keep your eyes open. The professor and I will meet you at the campsite. Remember the rules. Never lose sight of the road. Your gear is your life. Look after it. Respect the weather. Shelter, Water, Food. In that order. Don't tread on powder. Move at light, stay warm at night. Don't stare into the darkness, it will stare back."

The company carried on as the two grown men walked off into the forest, holding the slope of the mountain together. Wolflock frowned after them as they left. Something wasn't right. What if Thuthukta was Astraxis in disguise and he was about to murder their guide?

But that wouldn't do him any good. He'd also be lost in an unfamiliar mountain a day before Winter came in full force, with no supplies. Wolflock rubbed his arms and stayed close behind the wagon as it rolled on. It made more sense for the fiend to keep Sangur alive, so he had an expert to fall back on. He had no reason to try and attack anyone but Mothy and Wolflock. He ignored the surrounding conversations as they walked up the craggy mountain road, until he heard Etienne speak.

"What a pretty little trinket. Is it yours, Mothy?"

Wolflock turned to see the red-haired boy picking up one of Mothy's wooden statuettes with the opal eye glittering in the white snow.

"Huh? Oh! How did that fall out? Yes. Sorry, Etienne. Yes, it is mine."

"Did you make it?"

As Wolflock saw Mothy put it back in his bag, and he let go of the breath he held onto.

"I carved the crow, yes. An old friend of mine gave me the opals. She said they were enchanted to speak to one another when they're close."

"Speaking stones? That's powerful magic. Expensive too."

Mothy chuckled. "They don't really speak. They just glow and get warm. If you press them, they give you a sense of where the others are no matter how far away you are in the world."

"How sentimental. Hopefully, you'll be able to give them to someone when we make it to the castle. I must say, there are more than a few pretty and charming people up there."

"Oh, that's fine. I-"

"What do you mean when we make it?" Blayne sneered as they rounded the path and found themselves walking between cliffs a few minutes from the landing they would set up camp in. "Our guide has deserted us with the only person who could have survived this mess. We have no food, pitiful shelter, and no weapons to even try hunting with. We're all going to devolve into savages and eat each other!"

Wolflock snorted as he saw Mothy help Ms Pakuna and Shĭmìsī pluck up a clump of mushrooms and shake the spores back onto the tree roots to help more grow for next season. Fiddi called out from her seat any bird's nests she saw for them to inspect while Tareq gave each pine tree a shake to try and dislodge the cones. He had said that he'll drink pine needle tea, but he drew the line at eating them as food.

"I'd rather eat to be happy than full."

"I'll take you off the bark and pine needle menu for this evening, then," Mothy joked as he scrambled up the embankment to help the ladies climb out after him.

Even with no help from the Merris siblings and Blayne, the company amassed a bucket of rough food to prepare and boil up into a rustic stew.

"Perhaps my herbs and spices will come in handy this evening." Shĭmìsī skipped up to Wolflock with a grin that turned her cheeks into rosy apples. "This is much more fun than just walking and talking. I never knew there could be so much food in the wilderness. I'm going to have to rethink my approach to cooking in other countries. I'm going to need a lot of guides. What if I pick something that's poisonous?"

"First you test it on your wrist, then the inside of your lip." Mothy demonstrated with one of the wrinkled berries they'd found. "If it burns, blisters or stings, don't eat it."

"But chillies burn and sting," Tareq protested as he jogged up to them, arms full of pinecones.

The front wagon group debated what constituted a poison and a spice, as well as going over their own tales of how they were taught to identify them. It was the most interaction Wolflock had seen the company have, and it made him smile. Intelligent conversation without belligerence. If university held more of this, then he knew he'd be happy. He just had to get there. There was still no opportune moment to speak to Mothy about the lollies he'd kept in his pocket.

The company came to the open space between a path leading down into a thick forest and a rocky trail leading up to high white cliffs. Shĭmìsī lit the fire and boiled up their pine needles for a tea and to freshen up, allowing everyone to at least wash their faces, hands and feet while their forgeable medley brewed.

Thuthukta arrived back at sunset with a strange brown creature slung over his shoulder. Wolflock leaped to his feet, thinking he had Sangur, but it turned out to be an old mountain pig slung over his shoulder.

"Where is Sangur?" he asked, blocking Thuthukta's way to the campfire.

The professor stood like a mighty tree in front of Wolflock, surveying him up and down without expression, then jerked his thumb over his shoulder. Sangur trudged on behind the large man with a glum look. His coat hung from him in tatters and his belt was missing.

"What happened?" Wolflock ran up to the guide.

"I caught a rabbit," Sangur snapped. "But a bear wanted it more."

He had been lucky to escape with his life. The attack had left him with a few light scratches treated inexpertly by Etienne as Thuthukta and Shĭmìsī prepared the boar. Along with the spices she volunteered to lavish upon the meat and stew, they ate a hearty dinner. They even had enough stored for breakfast. It wasn't enough to feed eleven people for a week, but they only had one more day of travel. Wolflock had his regular cup of wild lettuce tea and shared it with Fiddi, Tareq and Shĭmìsī. He hoped Mothy would make some up as well, but he didn't get a chance to insist.

Wolflock watched as the lines in Sangur's face deepened while he looked over the map to the university.

"Is everything on track?" he asked the guide, procrastinating on asking Mothy for a private word.

Sangur sighed. "Yes. More or less. I thought we'd taken the wrong road, but, somehow, we've come back on track."

Fiddi looked at the map from the guide's other side. "Oh! I saw that, so I kept a close eye out on where the next landmarks were and fixed it. See here," she pointed to the map where a road wound back and forth across the front of the mountain, "I thought we were going to be travelling here, which is steep, but a faster route. That's the way we normally come and go from the university. But we missed the fork back here," she pointed just past the cave where they found the dead man. "Which led us all the way around the back of the mountain, but it's such a flat road that we're making great time. We'll be able to get back on track tomorrow morning."

Sangur still looked concerned, but Wolflock felt his chest lighten. They'd be out of Astraxis's grasp soon. One more sleep and they'd be hours from the university. And not with a moment left, judging by the icy wind announcing the Winter frost coming. He had to speak to Mothy. Wolflock made up his mind. He'd talk to Mothy as soon as he got up to go to bed, but he would wait until then.

"Will you sing for us on our last night, Sangur?" Blayne drawled, turning his nose up at the food. "No, I won't be eating that. It came from the ground."

Wolflock cocked his head to the side and looked around. Most of the other travellers made similar looks between one another, then burst out laughing.

"No. No, I haven't got the energy for it."

"Let me put a bit more pepper in this and that will give you some good qi to play with," Shǐmìsī tittered as she heaped in a spoonful of peppercorns.

Sangur watched her turn the bland mushroom stew into black fire and sighed. "You know what? I'll get my guitar after dinner. But, first, I have a spice I was waiting to use for the last night's lamb; I'm sure it will go well with this, too."

He took a little pouch from his boot and upended it into the pot. Shǐmìsī stirred it in and began dishing up everyone's dinner.

"I just want to say that this has been an unexpectedly pleasant trip and I look forward to studying with most of you." Tareq lifting his spoon in a toast.

Everyone else lifted their spoons, too, except Thuthukta, who raised up a silver fork.

"To bright minds and happy studies," he said, and everyone repeated it.

Wolflock eyed the fork in the light. It looked very familiar. An elegant wave design crept up the handle. It was a fork from the Silver Ice Hair!

As everyone else sat down, Thuthukta remained standing and stepped away from the fire.

"Rule number eight!" Blayne called after him.

"If the darkness wants to watch me, it's going to have more problems than me watching back," the professor grumbled and carried on towards the woods over the road.

Wolflock got to his feet as if he needed to relieve his bladder as well, but then thought that was a strange thing to do. But, then again, they were in mortal peril, so standing guard over such matters wasn't that strange. But he hadn't said anything before he stood up.

Feeling his skin burn red from embarrassment, he stood in limbo, neither going nor staying.

The group took up their bowls and started eating, except for Mothy, who dug through his bag for something. He pulled a jacket free and inside of it toppled out the crow statuette from earlier. He picked it up and looked around.

No.

Mothy's expression turned into a smile as he spotted Etienne.

No!

"I was wondering," Mothy began, raising the opal eyed crow to the terrible student doctor.

"NO!" Wolflock shouted.

The fire snapped into silence.

Mothy looked directly at him, eyes wide.

"You can't!" Hot tears filled his eyes.

His friend didn't speak.

"I'm your friend! Me! Not him! You can't want to give this fraud something so close to your heart!"

Etienne rolled his eyes. "Not this again-"

Mothy silenced him by getting to his feet. "How can you call yourself my friend?" His low voice felt like a boulder being thrown into Wolflock's chest.

"We have been through so much. I'm sorry! I'm sorry about the lollies. I didn't know what they would do but I knew it wouldn't hurt you. I would never do anything to hurt you. You're my best friend and I love you!"

"Then why do it? You say you didn't know what they did, but how can I trust that? You used the powder on that Najord boy and you've been carrying around samples of the ingredients to make that despicable filth! How can I trust you?"

Wolflock flinched. "I... But you can. I know well enough what might cause harm and I'd never-"

"You already did! They did the exact same thing back at the mill. You're no better than them!"

"Mothy, that isn't fair! I'm nothing like those monsters. Everything I did was to stop people from suffering the same way you did, and to save that little girl. To save Himi and the other mermaids. We did good things. We saved the Hunter's Guild children. Doesn't the ends justify the means?"

Mothy's clenched fists shook and his flaming black eyes stared at Wolflock like a demon mad with rage. "You fed me a drug without my knowledge. Without me saying it was fine! It should never have been an option in your mind, and the fact that you're arguing with me over my own feelings makes me wonder why I ever thought you were my friend in the first place! I hope I never see you again!"

Mothy kicked the stump he had been sitting on out of the way and stormed up the old craggy rock trail. Sangur groaned and chased after him.

Wolflock felt all eyes fall on him. The seething

indignation in their gazes burnt his pride and he felt it wither within him. Unable to say anything to the accusing eyes looking over him, he turned and slunk away into the woods where Thuthukta had disappeared into.

The cold wind whipped around him, crying through the trees. He had come so far. He'd learned so much. And, yet, here he was again. Humiliated. Friendless. And, this time, without anyone to save him.

He walked aimlessly along the little path through the trees until he stopped, hearing Thuthukta ahead of him. Wolflock rested his forehead on the tree and scrunched up his face. One train of thought told him Mothy just didn't understand.

But Mothy did understand. He understood better than anyone. Mothy had sacrificed much more than him to be here, and he'd come all this way trusting Wolflock was on his team.

No! He wasn't in any danger. Can't he see I'd never put him in any danger? Wolflock clenched his fist against the tree and held his breath. If there was ever a time he wished he could use magic it was now. He wanted to turn invisible or reverse time or just make everyone forget. But, then he would be as bad as Chestir, Volseggir, Najord and Astraxis. He had been just as bad as them, just with the pretence that it was for good.

A deep chuckle emanated from a little further in the woods, breaking Wolflock from his spiral. It sounded like someone talking to a baby or a pet. He wiped his eyes and walked forward, peeking around the pine tree. A dark figure squatted between trees and he wouldn't have been able to see them in the darkness if it hadn't been for two ethereal glowing foxes. One blue, one purple. They looked fluffier than normal foxes, with short, cute snouts, and large, watery eyes. The squatting figure giggled again as they tumbled around him, making noises like popping bubbles.

"Professor?" Wolflock frowned.

Thuthukta gasped and the two foxes vanished into glowing mist that flew into the bamboo cylinder.

"What are you doing?" the professor growled, marching up to Wolflock in the darkness.

"I... I'm not sure. What was that?"

"What was what?"

"That magic. I've never seen that before."

"It's just illusions, boy. Nothing more." The professor coughed.

Wolflock raised his eyebrow. "They looked very cute."

Professor Thuthukta cleared his throat and stood awkwardly in front of Wolflock. His stature, like a mighty tree, may as well have had maramuti swinging off him.

"Do they have names?"

The lecturer bit his lip and looked away before resting his hand on the bamboo cylinder. This was it. The moment of truth. He was either going to kill Wolflock right there and now with the swirling knife, or-

Professor Thuthukta twisted the cap off the cylinder, and the blue and purple clouds soared out and landed on the snow as the adorable fox pair, lighting up the space. The professors face wrinkled with pure joy as the foxes played together in front of him.

"Suki and Puki." He couldn't help but grin with perfect white teeth against his smiling lips.

Wolflock noticed beautiful, Xiayahn writing outlined their edges as if they were drawings. The illusion enchantment must have been on a scroll or something similar on the inside of the container. He hadn't seen so much expression on the lecturer's face since they'd met.

As he looked at the older man in the light of the magical foxes, he saw tiny trinkets he hadn't noticed. The inside of his thick jacket was lined with rows of tiny pins. He leaned forward to swirl the foxes and his jacket opened enough for Wolflock to see that the pins were brightly coloured flowers, costumed women, and single, Xiayahn words. They looked like cheap carnival tokens and prizes, but they were carefully pinned to a secret place close to his heart.

"You got this from Xiayah while you were on your holiday, didn't you?"

Thuthukta smiled. "You have an eye for detail, don't you, Mr Felen?"

"You teach something in the military department too, don't you?"

Again, he nodded. "I used to teach battle magic and tactics. After my accident, I teach ethics."

"Being surrounded by violence, history and political mistakes must be quite dark. This is all to give yourself balance, yes?"

One of the illusionary foxes started licking Thuthukta's hand and he giggled like a deep voiced child. "The fox festival is only held once every twelve years. I wasn't going to miss it for the world. Or the panda one. Or the rabbit festival."

All adorable fluffy creatures.

"And Sangur's rabbits from earlier. Rabbits aren't as clever as pigs. You deliberately didn't catch them. You opted for the old pig, which, I'll say, was as tough as boot leather."

Thuthukta's face fell. "I... I only killed the pig because I saw it limping and alone. It wasn't going to make it through the Winter. It was lucky it even crossed my path. I only intended on stripping a berry bush I saw at breakfast."

Wolflock sighed and squatted to swoosh the foxes, too. The lecturer had come along the North from Xiayah as well. There wasn't any way he could have been on the Silver Ice Hair for the past few months. "So, you're not Astraxis... You don't have a swirling, three bladed knife, do you? No purple powder?"

He expected Thuthukta to look confused and ask what he was talking about, but the broad man's face turned stony. "What did you just say?"

Wolflock couldn't respond. He opened his mouth to speak, but a ground shaking scream echoed through the trees.

"That's coming from the camp!" Thuthukta jumped to his feet and ran, his two glowing foxes leading the way.

Wolflock took off after him and, after a short run, they came back to find the campers still around the fire, looking hazily towards the path that led along the rocks.

"Where did the scream come from?" The professor barked at the group. Their slow, dazed response told them both something wasn't right.

"Pretty..." Shǐmìsī laughed and tried to touch the

glowing foxes.

Ms Pakuna pointed a shaking hand up the rock path.

"Mothy went up there. He might be in trouble."

They lost no time, taking off at a run. Wolflock lit his bone match and the foxes streamed around them, lighting the way and avoiding the cliff edges and trip hazards. Snow started cutting through the air as the wind picked up. The scream rang out again, much closer than before. The pair of them rounded a jagged corner and didn't know what they were seeing.

Sangur held his left hand on his thigh. He was injured and blood splattered the snow. A gust of wind pummelled them as the fjallarugal screamed and beat its wings. It was visible; a gigantic white bird with four wings spreading at least twelve feet across. It snapped its beak at Sangur and Wolflock thought it had attacked him, but there was no blood on its beak or foot long claws, which left deep gouges on the ground beneath it.

Wolflock threw his hand out and up to cast more light from the candle and saw the swirling knife behind the fjallarugal, dripping with blood.

In Mothy's hand.

All noise muted as his mental web broke.

Mothy? How could it have been Mothy?

The fjallarugal screamed again and stepped back. Mothy tried to dodge away from it, but it lifted its foot and gripped his arm with the knife. The monstrous bird beat its wings and lifted the blond boy off the ground.

"Mothy!" Wolflock choked and ran forward, but it was too late.

The fjallarugal took flight with his best friend in its talons. It took Mothy... and his knife.

CHAPTER 10

Guided to Evil

Wolflock ran up to the place Mothy had been snatched from and slipped, but Thuthukta's powerful hand grabbed his shirt collar and yanked him back. The lecturer held him steady, but Wolflock struggled to get free. Nothing made sense. Mothy?

"He's gone, Wolflock. There's nothing to be done. I'm sorry."

Wolflock's breath came in short sharp bursts, and he fell to his knees. "Mothy!" he screamed into the snow. Waves of tears tore through him harder than the blistering cold wind could. He looked up to where his friend had been taken from, and his breathing slowed, but remained just as ragged.

"Sangur? What happened?" Professor Thuthukta asked, keeping a hand on Wolflock's back.

"I came to make sure young Mothy didn't get separated from the group for long and then the fjallarugal attacked. Mothy pulled out the dagger and tried to attack me. I think he thought he could get rid of me and blame it on the bird. I got away from him, but not before he stabbed me in the leg."

Something glinted in the snow as one of the glowing foxes raced passed. Without thinking, Wolflock scrambled forward and snatched it up. The wooden crow with one opal eye. Thuthukta gripped him by the arm and hoisted him to his feet, keeping him close.

"Why would he do that?" the professor yelled over the wind.

Wolflock sank into his own mind and desperately tried to keep his mess of clues away from thinking of Mothy being the culprit. He'd been with him everywhere. He'd helped guard Parihaan and keep her alive. He was the only one to nearly die during the poisoning on the Silver Ice Hair. He hadn't left his side during the last three investigations. It couldn't be him. Mothy couldn't be Astraxis.

But why did he have the knife?

A puff of dirt rushed into his face and he rubbed his eyes to get it out. As he pulled his hands away he saw purple. He waited for the feeling of elation to kick in, but nothing happened. Sound dulled around him and he looked up, blinking, to see Sangur glaring down at him, his hands covered in purple powder that he'd drawn from a pinstripe pouch.

"Not my most potent, but it will have to do. Back to camp. Both of you."

Thuthukta walked numbly ahead, his one eye glazed over, and a dopey grin spreading over his face.

"Keep those foxes out," Sangur barked. His gruff tone vanished and Wolflock heard a silky voice cut through the wind.

Wolflock didn't feel compelled to move, but Sangur didn't know that. He followed the instruction, copying the professor. If he tried to run here he only had sheer cliffs and no light to escape with. He kept his breath steady.

Things weren't adding up. Mothy had the knife, Sangur had the powder. Why would their guide, the man who saved him from the fjallarugal, be using such a terrible powder? Unless he hadn't saved him from the fjallarugal at all. The first time it screamed was when he saw Astraxis come out of the wagon. Then again by the wagon when Sangur ran up to them. Prior to that it had been sitting on top of the goats watching them argue and dig through the cargo. Then it had found them in the grotto where Tareq had been attacked and lost his turban.

It wasn't the fjallarugal that attacked Tareq. It had been Sangur. He had been down in the grotto too and only let himself be known after Wolflock spotted him. Was he an agent for Astraxis? Or worse?

They reached the light of the campfire and Wolflock made eye contact with Fiddi, Tareq and Shĭmìsī. He gave them a wide eyed stare and hoped it told them to play along. Shĭmìsī giggled and squirmed in her seat, which was an odd reaction.

"Oooo! The pretties are back! Come here, pretties," she cooed to the foxes.

"Sit," Sangur growled and shoved Wolflock to his knees just beside the fire. "Girl," he barked at Shĭmìsī, "get me your knife."

She continued to giggle and gave him a spoon.

"A knife, idiot!"

With another titter she passed him a stick.

"Stupid cow. Move!"

He shoved passed her and started looking for a blade.

"What happened? Where's Mothy?" Fiddi whispered when Sangur was far enough away.

"The fjallarugal took him. I'm going to find him."

"What happened to the party?" Her wide brown eyes looked terrified.

"They've been poisoned. He is going to control you all. The wild lettuce tea from earlier makes us immune. I don't know what happened to Shĭmìsī, though."

"She wanted to celebrate with a little bottle of rice wine. No one else liked the taste."

Wolflock laughed through his nose and eyed Sangur cursing as he couldn't find a blade by the fire. He got to his feet and scrutinised them, making sure they looked sufficiently obedient before stalking over to the wagon. Wolflock saw the unique, geometric pattern to his shoeprints in the dirt around the fire.

"Fiddi, pass this on to Tareq and Shĭmìsī as she sobers up. Pretend to be under his influence like your life depends on it. Make sure the others stay warm and get to Mystentine. Let him think he's in charge and keep using the wild lettuce tea from the tin in the wagon."

"What about you?"

"I need to find Mothy. I need to know he's safe." I need to know why he has that knife.

"That's a terrible plan. It's snowing and it's windy and it's night. You're breaking at least four of the survival rules and no one will know where you are."

Sangur kicked the wagon in rage and tore open each tent in turn, looking for the ceremonial knives he knew Tareq had.

Wolflock gripped the one eyed crow in his hands tighter. He felt the delicate pull of fine threads coming from the statuette. The strongest came from the direction of Mothy's bag in his tent, the next strongest came from back down the road they had come from. "In Mothy's bag should be some more statuettes with opals in them. They may lead us back together. Otherwise, I'll see you when the term starts."

Fiddi hissed a protestation at him but stopped as Sangur made his way back over to the campfire with one of the antique, stone knives. Wolflock crawled through the snow close to the backs of the drugged campers, staying hidden behind the logs they sat on. Blayne sat on the edge closest to the road with a thick blanket draped around his shoulders. Wolflock drew shallow breaths as the cold burned his chest.

"Where is the little bastard?' Sangur snarled at Thuthukta and Fiddi. Wolflock carefully glanced over Blayne's log and saw Sangur's necklace reflect the firelight. The necklace had a knot over his chest, where his heart was.

Wolflock tensed every muscle in his body. He knew he'd have to run for it. Any second now Sangur would see him behind Blayne. He had to go. Sangur was going to kill him if he stayed. Mothy might kill him if he found him, but he'd rather risk his chances with his best friend.

He gripped the edge of Blayne's blanket and ran. The blond boy didn't budge as the cold washed around him.

"Get back here!" he heard Sangur scream, but his legs flew like the wind down the slope. He leaped over boulders which were bolstering the mountain, and gripped the crow in one hand and the blanket in the other. He focused with all his might on running with everything he had. The magnetic thread from the crow felt like an imaginary hope, but he kept running.

Sangur's heavy panting from behind was drowned out by the savage winds. Without the trees as shields, the blistering cold and ice sliced into him. He didn't know if Sangur had the ability to resist the cold, and the thought that he could be right behind him filled him with the fire to keep moving forward.

He cloaked himself in the blanket, but after a while

the wind forced the cold through it. He couldn't see where he was going. The wind and ice swirled around him like a tumultuous nightmare of howling and burning cold, making it impossible to see as he trudged through the snow for what felt like hours. He dragged his legs through the knee deep ice, heaving one step at a time. After some time he didn't feel as cold anymore, but his eyes didn't want to stay open.

"Mothy!" he tried to shout, but the hoarse call was swallowed by the wind. "Mothy!"

He wasn't going to give up. Wolflock was never going to give up. He couldn't. He needed answers.

He tried lighting his bone match, but the wind doused it immediately. Over and over he tried to light it, but his fingers felt like sharp frost was growing inside them, and he had to tuck his hands under the blanket, guided only by the thin thread.

"Mothy!" he shouted, but it came out as a whisper.

The warm little thread grew thicker and Wolflock drew up the last of his energy to run to it. He hit something hard and fell backwards in the snow. The warm, opal thread led up the rocks he'd run into. Wolflock reached up, but found no way to ascend it.

"Mothy!" he called once more, tears freezing on his cheeks.

He dropped to his knees and hunched over in the snow, closing his eyes and wishing with all his might that things could be different.

"Mothy. I'm sorry..."

A heavy darkness enclosed Wolflock's consciousness and he wondered if that sound was the beating of his heart. It sounded like wings.

Rhiannon D. Elton

CHAPTER 11

Hatching a Plan

Wolflock had never considered what death would feel like. At the funerals he had to attend after the war, he was always told that those that passed would go back to Mother Pelaia, and they would take their lessons with them. They stayed in her Summerland until they were ready to return, and then their spiritual magic would come back as something, or someone, new.

He never thought the Summerland would have such a hard ground or be so soft, fluffy above. Or smell like poultry.

So they lied, he scoffed to himself. You do feel

pain when you're dead. Why is it so dark?

Wolflock stretched his creaky fingers and rolled over. His arm bumped a smooth round boulder, and, for a moment, he saw stars, but the fluffy sky above him nestled down and blocked them from view. Something grabbed his shins and pressed up against him. He thought he was warm until they straightened the blanket over the top of them both.

"Even on death's door you won't do as you're told," Mothy's voice muttered, but Wolflock could hear a smile in his voice.

"I'm not dead?" he asked into the darkness.

"You're awake. Thank goodness. You stopped shivering and I thought you were going back into hypothermia. Have you got all your fingers? I couldn't see in the dark."

Wolflock checked his hands, his mind still hazy. "Yes. Ten fingers and my toes are still in my shoes."

They both fell silent as Wolflock's mind collected itself.

"I'm sorry, Mothy."

His friend sighed, his body tensing.

"I know what I did was wrong. I just... I just do things without thinking about anyone else. In Plugh, that was how everyone I knew operated. They'd do whatever it took to get ahead, and they used people as rungs in the ladder to their perceived success. I feel like my sister's friend, Ginia, was the only one who didn't do things like that."

Still no response, so Wolflock continued.

"I'm not trying to make an excuse. I only wanted to explain. You're right. I sank to the same level as Najord when I used that powder to get answers from him. I was reckless with so many things coming up here and I thought that, because I have an innate curiosity, no matter the consequences, that everyone else must have it too. I drank Parihaan's drinking alcohol to see why she was addicted to it and I let Dr Växtadlare test the purple powder on me so we could test the antidote. That doesn't... it doesn't give me the right to do that to anyone else. Especially without telling them. I acted like a villain and I'm sorry."

"You're right," Mothy said. "You're always right. It's frustrating, you know?"

Wolflock gave him a shaky laugh. "It's a blessing and a curse."

His friend fell silent again and they listened to the soft cooing of the fjallarugal above them.

"I never meant to upset you, and I definitely never meant to lose your trust. You're the only true friend I've ever had and you have every right to hate me for what I did. I swear to you, I will never do anything like that ever again to friend or foe. If you ever want to be friends again, I'll be here." His throat clenched and he desperately tried to stop the hot tears in his eyes. "I'll not push the subject or annoy you anymore."

In response, Mothy hugged Wolflock's shins and Wolflock hugged Mothy's back.

"You're the worst," he heard Mothy cough. "I wanted to join you the moment you caught the whiff of a mystery, and you kept pushing and pushing. I couldn't resist. I even started taking my own clues. You're a terrible influence, Lockie."

Wolflock's heart burst with radiant joy as Mothy used his nickname.

"Tell me about your clues in a moment. But, I have to clarify something. We are under the fjallarugal, yes?"

Mothy laughed. "Oh yeah. Snowball. She's been eating the lice off the goats. I stopped her from eating all the food in the cart, but she kept sneaking back. She's basically impossible to see against anything white."

"That explains so much. When did you know she was safe?"

Mothy thought for a moment. "I think when I first

saw her on the goats on our second night. Her colours are very strong and, when she saw Sangur, the little red beams of anger and aggression were only directed at him. When she chased you, she was trying to pluck you up and keep you safe. The same way she did with me tonight."

"She saw Sangur kill the man in the cave. She knew since then that he was dangerous and she's been trying to keep us safe. By the gods it all makes sense now. That's strange though... Sangur and Urgi said when they first told us about the fjallarugal that she was dangerous, but I saw them wink at each other as if they knew she wasn't. Do you think that her seeing him murder that man made her hostile to him?"

"Maybe. The clean air on the mountain and the white snow is making the colours I see around people brighter."

"Your eyes have been more expressive, too. They've been changing colour vividly."

"Hah. Well, you're out of luck trying to see them under Snowball at the moment. I can see you, though." He hugged Wolflock's shins again. "Sangur's colours have changed, though. When we did the induction and he told us the story he had a solid earthy green colour. It felt... certain. Now, he has this wispy black smoke around him like he's trying to hide, and, even when he smiles, there are blood red spikes that try to stab out at anyone around him. It's frightening."

"He's not who he says he is. He used the purple powder in the soup tonight and he blew it in my face and Thuthukta's face."

"I saw you drinking the wild lettuce tea."

Wolflock chuckled. "It's habit for me, now. I shared it with Shĭmìsī, Tareq and Fiddi. Before I left, I told Fiddi to play along with him and keep the others safe. Hopefully, they'll all be out from under his influence when we meet up with them. Did he injure you?"

Mothy tensed again. "No. He followed me up the mountain and started asking about what we knew and the slave trading cell we dismantled. I told him little bits and pieces, but he wasn't there to try and make me feel better. He was there for him.

"When he realised he couldn't get anything else out of me, he said bad slaves need to be made an example of, and tried to stab me. I dodged it and kicked the knife out of his hands. Snowball came to my rescue as I snatched up the knife. Sangur tried to grab it back, but I flung it out and caught his leg, then slid under Snowball. She kept me safe until you arrived."

"Seeing you with that wretched knife ruined all my theories and clues. Then I thought this giant pigeon had taken you for dinner."

"No," Mothy chuckled. "She just got spooked seeing the three of you there. I was worried for a bit that she would feed me to her babies, but they're still egged."

Wolflock smiled, closing his eyes and enjoying the soothing warmth of the fjallarugal nest.

"What are we going to do, Lockie?"

"We're going to stop Sangur, who I suspect may be closely linked to Astraxis, and put him in the custody of the Mystentine University Guard with all our evidence."

Mothy snickered, "Ha. Mug. M, U, G is mug... Haha."

Wolflock laughed along with him and thought about a plan. "Do you still have the knife?"

"Mmmhmm. It's not very useful. Good for puncturing I suppose, but not for slashing or cutting much."

"It cut my rope on the Silver Ice Hair pretty well, thank you."

"Oh yeah... I forgot about that."

"Our focus should be on getting him away from the others so we can capture him. If we wake up early we'll be able to follow the stars and set our trap where the road reaches the one we were originally meant to take."

Mothy chuckled again. "I heard Fiddi messed up his plans by getting us back on track. She's clever. I like her. And Shĭmìsī. I hope the food at the university is as good as her cooking. Let's get our plan together in the morning."

They both yawned back and forth, unable to keep their eyes open any longer.

"Mothy?"

"Mmm?"

"Thank you. I don't know what I'd do without you."

Wolflock felt Mothy's cheek tense as he smiled next to his calf. "Don't make me mad at you again. I missed you, too."

CHAPTER 12

The Journey Ends

The bright white glow woke Wolflock up first. He had to open his eyes slowly in order to adjust to the dawn light illuminating the canopy of feathers above him. He saw his friend still sleeping, his arms and legs twisted in all manner of unnatural angles.

Wolflock got to his hands and knees, made sure the blanket stayed over his friend, and crawled to the edge of the giant nest. The fjallarugal's nest of feathers, fur and sticks were woven so tightly together that Wolflock understood why it could withstand the storm they endured last night. He came to the edge and climbed up the curve, pushing the feathers out of the way until his head popped out the side and he could see the clear morning.

The sun hadn't risen, but, because no clouds lingered after last night's snowstorm, the sky stretched a dusty blue over them, only the brightest stars still shining. He looked up to try and see the giant bird and saw its beady, black eyes turn down to look back.

The pristine white feathers reached all over its enormous body and its overall shape resembled that of a chicken. Without warning, it dropped its head down and its huge beak knocked him back down under the feather ceiling. The fjallarugal kept coming for him, pecking and picking at his hair. It didn't hurt. It was just very pushy. Like a mother hen grooming a chick.

As quickly as it started, it stopped and withdrew its head back outside. Mothy groaned as he stretched his arms and flopped back into the nest.

"She's going to let us leave, right? I don't fancy being fed by a fjallarugal."

"I'm sure she's a great cook," Mothy responded, stretching again. "What's the plan?"

"When I saw the map yesterday, Fiddi mentioned that we would be joining back up with the original road today after breakfast." He picked up a stick from the nest and drew a rudimentary map on one of the eggs nestled nearby. The brown of the stick left markings, but it didn't damage the hard casing. "This is where the road meets University Rise. There's a little woodland at the junction."

"If we go there now, we will be able to search the area for a place to set up our trap."

"Exactly. Do you think Snowball here could carry us? Help us get a head start?"

Mothy laughed, "I don't know how to steer a fjallarugal."

Wolflock smirked. "Do you want to try?"

As Snowball fidgeted more and more, the boys could tell she wanted to move. They climbed out of the nest and crawled onto her smooth back, trying not to pull out any feathers. They used their combined strength to tear the blanket in order to make loops to go around her front wings. The blanket was too small to create reigns, so Wolflock threaded his trouser belt through Mothy's so they would stay fastened together, but still have full use of their arms. Snowball flapped both sets of wings in agitation as they boys made sure their loops were firm.

While in their precarious position, they waited for her to move.

"Snowball?" Wolflock tapped his heels on her side like he would a horse. "Can we get moving, now? The sun is about to rise and we're on a schedule."

"I don't think she cares about schedules, Lockie."

"Well, she's going to care about ours." Wolflock tapped her again, but to no avail. He tried tugging on some of her feathers, but she just turned her head and eyed him like an irritable aunt.

Wolflock let out a loud scream as if he were frightened, hoping that would move her. She ignored him. Mothy joined in.

"What if we sang?"

They didn't need to. The beating of wings drew nearer and another fjallarugal soared up to the nest, grooming Snowball's face and neck.

"That's got to be the father," Wolflock grinned, pointing at the glittering stream of blue feathers cascading from his head and tail.

The boys laid flat on Snowball's back as she wiggled out of the nest, allowing room for the father to nestle in, keeping the eggs warm. Her wings twitched and she dropped off the edge of the cliff. Wolflock's stomach leaped into his throat as they plunged. Snowball flapped her four sail-like wings and they rose into the sky. All the boys could do was hold on with all their might.

"Mothy! Mothy look! The university! I can see it from here!" he shouted, gripping onto Snowball's back feathers with one hand as the beating of her wings threatened to shake them both off.

He could see above them as, at the peak of the mountain, there came flashes of brilliant light, as well as smoke from fireplaces and chimneys. He could only imagine how wonderful it all seemed.

"I'm gonna be sick." Mothy grimaced. "It was better when she had me by the arm."

"We've got to steer her to the left and down, so she lands."

"We didn't think about how to get her to land!"

Wolflock made an apologetic face, making Mothy's expression look even more concerned. The blond boy yanked his blanket rope with a squawk, and Snowball jolted to the side.

"Too much! Too much!"

Wolflock pulled his rope, but, with both of them pulling, Snowball soared directly up. She kept going and the boys screamed, their muscles locking in place as she looped completely over. Wolflock's shouts of fear quickly turned into excited hoots as they flattened out.

"That was amazing!"

Mothy's bright blue eyes stayed stuck wide.

"There! That's the path." Wolflock nodded and loosened his rope, steering Snowball left.

The three of them soon learned what each of them meant by their pressure and movements, and the fjallarugal became used to the ropes quickly. They weaved left and right, following the slowly ascending path all the way to the woodlands before the junction of trails.

"How do we get down?" Mothy shouted over the wind.

Wolflock hadn't thought about this step until now. He had a stupid idea that just might have been brilliant enough to work.

"Keep hold of the rope and jump off."

Mothy couldn't speak. The notion was so crazy he couldn't even respond.

"We'll die," was all he managed to say.

Wolflock looked down. Yes. Yes they would.

"I have a better idea then! Pull the ropes and we'll do a loop, but, when she finishes the circle, keep them taut so she plummets, then let go with enough time to let her correct."

"I like that more, but not much more."

Wolflock laughed and waited a few more moments until they flew over the woods. "Now!"

Snowball's shoulders tensed and she pulled her nose up, flapping against the winds that buffeted her. She curved in a wide crescent and the boys hung on to her feathers. Wolflock felt his legs start to fall from her back just as she came to the end of the curve and nosedived towards the road.

"Lockie?" Mothy's voice trembled as the ground rushed to them. "Lockie?"

Not yet.

"Lockie, when?"

Three, two... one!

"Now!" Wolflock shouted, relaxing the blanket rope and letting Snowball flap her wings hard enough to align herself with the ground and slow down.

She flapped so hard that it tore the blanket from his aching hands. He tried to grip the feathers, but one came out in his hands and Snowball bucked. Wolflock felt himself fly into the air and Mothy followed, still clinging to the blanket rope for their lives.

Snowball turned right and spiralled into a thicket of trees. Wolflock fumbled with his belt, able to unlatch it just in time to drop into the snowy arms of a pine tree before it bashed into him. The giant white bird flapped, throwing Mothy around like a rag doll, and, finally, landed on the top of the tree, bending it down with dangerous creaking noises. His friend lightly touched the snow before letting go of the blanket rope and popping safely to the ground. Wolflock fell out of the tree and groaned, thankful the snow was soft.

Snowball pecked at the blankets and nudged them off her beautiful wings before taking flight and vanishing into the dawn sky. As she flapped, she blew snow off the ground within the clearing, revealing some not quite dormant bushes and an old hunters pit.

"A bit unceremonious to not wait for thanks," Wolflock grunted, rubbing his side.

"I... do not like flying," was Mothy's response. "What now?"

Wolflock grinned. "I have scarcely been given the gift of planning time, so I am going to thoroughly enjoy this."

They got to work. The place Snowball had left them in was a perfect clearing to lay their trap. Mothy made a rudimentary sign post and stuck it into the middle of the road. Wolflock's plan was to guide Sangur to the clearing, get him talking for long enough to obtain a confession, and organise the travelling party to assist in his capture. Wolflock smirked to himself as he worked, because he had plenty he could talk to the guide about.

The sign post in the middle of the road was a basic arrow sign, but on it was carved the Xed eye, pointing Sangur in the direction of trees pinned with all the letters Wolflock had folded into his journal. Letters from

Chestir, Volseggir, Lord Therym and Najord were all pinned to the trees leading to the clearing. Empty pouches with traces of purple powder, sketches of the ephedra he'd tried to poison Parihaan with, and, when they ran out of clues, they kept carving the symbols for the slaves and the names of the people he'd hurt. He stabbed the swirling knife into the tree behind the old hunter's pit and recovered it with sticks and as much snow as he could.

Wolflock was glowing with pride at their set up. It was perfect.

Now to wait.

They waited by the road, unable to make a fire without any equipment, and looked for berries, herbs and mushrooms they could eat raw while they waited. Time dragged on for what felt like an eternity. Wolflock paced back and forth, still unable to see how Sangur could be linked to Astraxis. He went over his mental web, but the sheer amount of evidence he'd accumulated over the past few months cluttered his mind.

He hated waiting.

After another few hours of waiting, they heard the clatter of the wagon and the grunting of the huge goats. Mothy hid himself off the road and Wolflock ran to the clearing and stood in position.

He folded his arms and leaned against the tree, then changed his mind and stood with his arms crossed, head down and feet wide apart. That didn't feel natural either. Pacing back and forth with his chin pinched in his fingers, he considered what would be the best look to meet his nemesis. Wolflock put his hands behind his head and blew a raspberry.

"Come now. You played this game with Myna all the time." He skipped from foot to foot and shook his hands. "Just the biggest case of your life getting solved right here and now. That's fine. I'm fine. Everything is fine."

His nerves prickled up and down his spine and Wolflock practised his first words to the fiend.

"Your time is over. No. Stop there, villain! No. Look at all these clues you left me. Hmm... getting closer. Thanks for making this easy. I mean... it's a lie, but still."

"I'm going to end you."

"A bit too dark for what I was going for. Thank you for coming, Sangur. But I really don't feel right calling you by that name, since you killed him and all."

Sangur didn't even blink. He just stared with cold grey eyes.

"You did confirm you have close ties to the mastermind behind all this, though. There's just a few things I'd like to put together."

"Why? What's been your interest in all this? And how have I confirmed anything?"

"Let's start from the beginning, shall we?"

Sangur rolled his eyes and drew out a pipe. "You're going to keep talking while all your friends are dying in the cold? I knew you were heartless, Lockie, but I didn't expect this."

A thread snapped into place in Wolflock's mind. Very few people had ever called him Lockie, and only those who had been on the Silver Ice Hair did it with any natural tones like Sangur just did. His silky voice, although a bit muffled by his flowing blond beard, also seemed uncannily familiar.

"You were hiding in the chest on the wagon for the first day, weren't you? I mean, my questions are rhetorical, so you don't have to answer them. I already know. But if you feel the need, please confirm or deny anything."

"This is an ego stroke for you, is it?"

"Oh yes. Anyone could tell you that. I'm the cleverest person I know, and to have someone challenge me for a few months has been riveting." Wolflock glanced around the clearing, hoping Sangur would walk forward just a few more steps into the pit, but he stopped and smoked as if he were bored.

"How did you know we were travelling up the mountain? You must have spoken to Chestir, right?"

Sangur sneered. "Such an idiot. Leaving clues children could find him with. Never trust someone via long distance. Letters can be very promising until you arrive and find everything in tatters."

"Ah. I suppose that was the same with Lord Therym, Najord and Volseggir, then? The only ones you met that were your agents were Faleen, Bleen and Parihaan then?"

Sangur's eyes flicked up to him with a warning look.

"Oh! I recognised the pinstripe pouch you have. One identical to it was sent to Faleen and Bleen by one Mr Gilmere. And, of course, you left me the letter about Parihaan drinking all the alcohol she smuggled. That was what gave you away in the end, you know? You kept leaving me evidence that pointed to the extensions of yourself and your business. As I closed in you tried to divert me from seeing you by showing me someone you were attached to.

"Anyway, so you realised we were going up the mountain, your business was in tatters and disintegrating even more, what else could you do but seek revenge?

You couldn't just join the party because Mothy and I knew your face well, which is why you killed the real Sangur and stole his snuffle to take his place. Isn't that right, Astraxis? Or should I say... Stra?"

Sangur blinked slowly and sighed with an evil smile. He then reached up and pulled off the fur hat and a blond snuffle he had attached around his face. Where its face had been under the hat was covered in purple powder.

"Now, this I have to know. How did you know it was me?"

Wolflock scoffed, seeing the intricate web of clues straighten out, everything falling into place. "I know what a snuffle looks like. Sangur's beard grew too poorly to cope with the cold weather, so he used a snuffle. There was an oval mark on the back of his head from where it was attached. But snuffles are loyal creatures, so I didn't know until all the other clues made it the only viable option."

Stra smiled contemptuously as he paced back and forth in front of the pit, eyeing the knife stuck in the tree beside Wolflock.

"You also cut through Sangur's compass. The only one that opened with a map. I could tell by the location of the knot you've used to retie it. You couldn't tie the wagon knots to save your life, you refused to play the guitar, you made sure the only person who knew Sangur well enough stayed behind with the body, the gloves on the stripped body covered his hand tattoos that would have identified him, and your shoe prints are as distinctive as your knife."

Stra continued to pace like a panther, his face contorting from contempt to fury. "Why pursue any of this though? I would have left you alone if you'd not stuck your nose into my business. You could have gone on your merry way without any issue."

Wolflock looked around the clearing again, but there was no sight of anyone arriving. He had to keep Stra talking.

"You tried to kill my friend. You saw his slave brand when he ran around the deck shirtless one day and you knew he'd be able to identify the signs of slavery, ruining one of the biggest branches of your nefarious business. You tried to blame the maramuti in the end. You even poisoned yourself to draw my suspicions away from you. I remember you doing it. You put the powder on your steak that day in the kitchen. You tried to influence Nan Ji's medicines, but Nü was too smart for you."

"I knew that little upstart was too clever for her own

good. She wouldn't even touch my herbs when I tried to give them to her."

"You used the Silver Ice Hair crew and company as subjects to experiment your terrible concoctions on, but, when the crew had the sickness scare, you had to stop. It took you a few weeks, but, after your stock of drinking alcohol was discovered and poured into the river, you practised with incense. Just because it was a different delivery method didn't make it any better though. The twins abused it the same way Parihaan abused the drinking alcohol. And the same way Najord, Lord Therym and Volseggir abused the powder as well."

"All pitiful idiots. Useless, good for nothing slugs. Worthless, pathetic fools!" Stra barked, pacing faster and staring at the knife with hunger in his eyes.

"You kept trying to get Mothy and I alone, though. You asked us to join you for tea at Irid, but the Captain was on to you. He kept me away, which made Mothy go off on his own to other places. Then you wanted to share a carriage from Creast to Mystentine. Although generous at the time, I see now it was only to get rid of us however you could."

Stra launched himself forward, unable to take the humiliation any longer. Wolflock smirked and watched as Stra's face paled as he broke through the snow and fell into the hunter's pit.

"Rule number six," Wolflock laughed, squatting down by the edge of the pit. "Never walk on pure powder. You'll fall through it and freeze to death, only to be found when the frost thaws in Spring."

Stra groaned and got to his hands and knees.

"You know, I knew you were here because of a few other things too, though. You use a lot of the stimulant herb ephedra. I found it around one of your crates in the Silver Ice Hair hull. Then, again, on Parihaan before she fell into a coma. I also recognised it on the wagon here. I haven't seen anyone else use it before, so it stood out. Then there was the fork you gave Professor Thuthukta. I remember he commented on the beautiful design. Trouble is, you stole it from the Silver Ice Hair. I spent so many hours cleaning those forks. I'd know them anywhere."

Wolflock walked around the rim of the pit and looked at the footprints in the snow leading up to it.

"But it's your shoes that give you away. The tread of your shoes was on the stairs where Parihaan fell, on my pillow at the Mermaid's Paddle, and at Tareq's turban where he was attacked. Your urge to stand out was always what was going to give you away."

Stra looked down, his shoulders dropped and in a

defeated voice, he said, "So, what now?"

"I guess we wait for the company to arrive and you'll be taken up to the university and handed over to the authorities."

"I have to stay in this pit until then? That's undignified."

Wolflock scoffed. "What's undignified is knowing you're destroying peoples lives, but you persist anyway."

"Oh, come off. Every wealthy family owns slaves, and they have too much money for their own good. They want to spend it one stupid things. I'm just fulfilling a supply in the market."

Wolflock's nose wrinkled in disgust. "You're a cretin and I'm glad you're in a hole."

The thumping of wings blew the snow off the trees as Snowball returned, pecking Wolflock's hair to groom him again.

"I'm glad you're not mad, Snowball. Look. We got the bad guy."

"Bad is a matter of perspective," Stra scoffed, but Wolflock had had enough. He was secure in the pit, so the dark haired boy walked around the clearing to clear the revulsion he felt for the monster in the hole.

He wondered why Mothy hadn't come back yet. Were the others still sick? Had something happened?

He couldn't leave Stra alone, but he also needed to know where the others were.

As he looked down the path of clues that led Stra right to him, he heard Snowball sneeze. The sound was adorable, but echoed, as if her head was in the pit. He whipped her head around and saw her purple dusted face come out of the pit with Stra gripping onto her beak. She dropped him on the ground and he glared at Wolflock.

"Kill him," he ordered.

The fjallarugal screamed and raced towards him. Wolflock dodged between the trees on the edge of the clearing, feeling Snowball's beak snap hard behind him. In the corner of his vision he saw Stra wrench the knife from the tree and start heading back to the blonde snuffle and hat he'd thrown on the ground. Wolflock slid under Snowball's legs, confusing the giant chicken, and ran to Stra. He had to put him back in the hole. He had to secure him. He couldn't let the monster of a man get away. He couldn't let him hurt Mothy again.

Wolflock tackled the wiry man around the middle and they both toppled downward. Before he could stab Wolflock, the knife flew from Stra's hand and clattered to the bottom of the pit. Both of them hung onto the snowy ledge, desperately trying to climb back out. The giant fjallarugal gathered her beady eyed bearings and looked around for Wolflock, intermittently scraping her face on the snow and trees to brush away the powder.

He tried to dig his foot into the pit wall and heave himself out, but the dirt just slipped out from under his foot when he pressed down.

"Lockie!"

Mothy and the others ran down the path, looking at the scene that only Mothy understood. He reached into his pocket and dug through it. Wolflock hoped to the gods of the mountain that he wasn't reaching for a weapon. He'd rather see Mothy run than be eaten by a bird he liked. Stra hoisted himself out to his waist and wriggled out of the hole. The others froze in fear and confusion, but Mothy kept running. Snowball screamed again, flapping all her wings in a frenzy as she raced towards Wolflock.

"Lockie! Catch!"

Mothy threw a bottle into the air. It bounced off the fjallarugal's wing and soared over Wolflock's head into the pit. Just in time he reached back and caught it, just as the giant bird snapped her beak down on his entire arm.

She clenched down hard and threw her head back, tossing him into the air and trying to gobble him whole.

"Snowball! No!" Mothy screamed.

Wolflock saw the terrifying inside of the bird's wet throat and heard Stra's mad laughter.

Then, everything stopped. The fjallarugal stopped, the laughter stopped.

Snowball leaned forward and vomited Wolflock out, the empty antidote vial from Dr Växtadlare's apothecary still clutched in his hand.

"Wh-what?" Stra stammered. "No. No! You-She should have eaten you!"

Wolflock wiped the bird's saliva from his face and arms, pulling a face. The smell was foul. Even through the terrible odour, he couldn't help but grin.

"She should have. Yes. But we've been able to block you at every path, Stra. We have antidotes to your powders and concoctions, and everyone who is ever at risk of being used by you or your people will have it at the read."

"This is impossible!" the bald man roared. The swirling, three bladed knife in his hand shook and he made one step towards Wolflock. "I will not be made to look like a fool by an insolent boy who doesn't know how to keep his nose out of other people's business!"

Wolflock saw the tall dark professor step quietly up behind Stra. He knew he'd won. From all sides, he had played his move and Stra had nowhere to go now he was caught in the web of clues the amateur sleuth had built for months.

"A bit late for that," Wolflock laughed, his smile not dropping as Stra growled.

The thin bald man launched forward to attack, but Professor Thuthukta stepped up and smacked him up the back of the head with the bamboo cylinder, knocking him out cold.

Mothy threw his arms around Wolflock and the company cheered. Snowball backed away, confused.

"That was the craziest thing I have ever seen," Blayne snorted. "You're both mad men."

"I can't believe she nearly ate you. Wild." Mothy grinned, wiping the bird mucous off his chest as a chorus of questions burst from the company.

"Is that the fjallarugal?"

"Who is that man?"

"Where is Sangur?"

"What a cute little snuffle!"

Thuthukta tied Stra's wrists and ankles before putting him in the chest he had smuggled himself into the travelling group with.

It was over.

* ~ * ~ * ~ * ~ * ~ *

The company was all too eager to hear the story of how they survived the snowstorm, met the fjallarugal, and found out who had murdered the real Sangur. Shĭmìsī made their final meal a banquet while they regaled the group with all of the clues they had found along the way.

But, just telling the story of the mountain's monster wasn't enough, they all wanted to hear more. While they spoke, Ms Pakuna jotted down everything she could in order to keep her trembling to a minimum. Wolflock and Mothy took them all the way back to when he first boarded the Silver Ice Hair months ago. They finished their early lunch just as Urgi arrived with two mountain guards.

"Thank goodness you're safe!" She cried. "We realised too late that Sangur was the one who had been killed. We tried to find you on the road, but you'd gone the wrong way."

"Fiddi helped get us back on track." Wolflock explained.

"We've been searching for you all for two days now. I cannot tell you how relieved I am that he didn't do away with you all. I've heard such terrible things from the guard about him now. Thank goodness it's all over."

The company set off again and each of them got to tell their own version of what they'd seen and how the fake Sangur had treated them as they trundled up the last road of their journey. Wolflock thought it was aptly named "University Rise".

Urgi's last sentence echoed in his mind as he walked alongside Mothy. His best friend saw his expression and elbowed his arm to wake him from his contemplation.

"Sentus for your thoughts?"

"Hmm? Oh. Stra said he wouldn't be made a fool of."

"Hah. You proved that wrong," Mothy laughed scornfully.

"You can only be made a fool of if you think someone is watching. What if there is someone else he answers to?"

They walked at the front of the group and turned a hairpin corner in the road. All breath was squeezed from their lungs by the majesty of the giant stone walls before them. The gates to Mystentine University stood just ahead of them with the old castle towering over the Northern edge.

"Lockie, you've spent months saving people. You have finally won. Stra, Astraxis, the mysterious A; he's gone. If there is someone on another level attached to him, we'll find them together. But, right now," he gripped

Wolflock's shoulders and steered him to the decorated stone walls, "I want you to look at this."

The clouds of doubt parted around his heart and mind as he looked at the magnificent inscription above the shining brass gates.

Mystentine University: Shared Wisdom Through Knowledge.

"We've made it." Wolflock whispered.

"Only once we get through those gates, my dear appraising investigator." Mothy puffed out his chest.

"Well then, let's step over the threshold, Dr Enitnelav."

Mothy pinched his chin the same way Wolflock normally did. "You know what, I think I might go by Dr Mothy. Just to be different."

"Scandalous. I like it."

The Case of the Mountain's Monster

Dixt Myna,

Wix gemaOt is. Wix analggiO gaft zu dex chen sax
dex mexg. Mathg exfist miO zu mittelen da thex zagen
fxObelen txeff. Wix ains altzat ain dex sexgalten blucx exflax
chlebxum gix anftimt sain ain aale bunden und aOtget. T bin
mehx betxeffent Ubax as dex aOnitfte iz ahentet. T hate it
kannen fange ain neuen behexxaO aOngel.

T Hate Leate ainen getaunten beaOäftigt. Wix absOtet
ainen sexsatz zu cxaffen ain atalaaft zalt, sexnatOxt ainen
sexhast piOeln aOlugele betxek, und anbalten dex Hexatellung und
sexlauf aain ain fuxOtbaxO atulbex. T kannen niOt gaxt zu za
aiO dex akademettat hilft niOt befugntat aain folgexang aam
gibmatux und untexauO.

T gixst zaOnen da ain laxte aam dex aOlebbuxt naO T
hate exfexaOt is. Und da niOt muthes fxagen. T bin niOt
ahentet zu let da mittelen miO sex zu at fxeunde aam. Mathg
und T aind ahentet zu tallen ain zummex. MiO neun anaxb iz
LLL. B untexbumft, Wibmatux untexbxingunge, Mgatentine
Uttademattat.

GiO iz saxta? GiO iz Flugt? T da niOt sexmiOt is, abex T
gixst zage, naO alle diex T da sexmiOt da. Bitte gaben thexm
miO iga. Und da hate biaex at apatzen Bxennan. T gixst niOt
baxten thexm anux bebalnt axing axuxaO T bin niOt is.

Dein bessthe,

Wolflud J. Selen.

About the Author

Rhiannon is the walker between worlds. One foot in Earth, the other constantly stepping into Pelaia. As if gazing into a crystal ball, she sees this other world and all that happens within it with the clarity of someone staring through a veil. It is her purpose in life to transcribe these histories, adventures and mysteries for you to enjoy.

This witchy woman was raised by a fairy who taught her that there are all kinds of magic throughout the world. She taught Rhiannon to withhold judgement because you never truly know another's story. She also taught her that everyone, no matter how flawed, has something to give.

The adventures of Rhiannon's youth lead her through trials and dangers that taught her about the darkness within the world, but it also showed her that anything could be overcome. There was always a way. Surrounded by so much apathy and hopelessness, Rhiannon made it her goal in life to show others the light and that if they could dream it they could do it.

The way she was shown this was through stories.

Stories of friendship, love, adventure, discovery, compassion, understanding, and kindness. All of these stories gave her new friends, new lessons, new life.

In the depths of her darkest place during year 11 and 12, when she felt at her loneliest, drugs surrounded her life in terrible ways, the self worth of those she loved and admired crumbled, she was relentlessly bullied and felt friendless in her most trying years, she lived in squalor due to bureaucratic errors, and yet she still had to be "perfect". She had to perfectly excel in school, she had to perfectly remain calm and gentle in the face of abusive men, she had to be a perfect role model for all those around her. That craving for perfection in order to get love nearly killed her several times. In all of this darkness with politicians sacrificing real people and real environments for imaginary money, with teachers displaying no compassion for their students, with men abusing women and children, with communities vilifying those who needed them most, with injustice reigning and all hope seemingly lost... Puinteyle was born.

All of these pains in life were fixed in Puinteyle.

All of them were able to be mended and healed because of a conscientious effort. The people of Puinteyle wanted to be better than their problems. Puinteyle was where people made an effort to love freely and always sought to help each other, animals and the environment. Harmony. True and beautiful harmony. Where the pendulum never swayed too far away from that beautiful harmonious and happy point of balance.

But like in our lives, there is always obstacles to overcome and darkness to understand. Therefore, Puinteyle would always have its own inner turmoils to learn and grow from too. Thus, the stories never truly end.

Rhiannon has always lived and breathed stories, knowing her role in life is to be this guide through a new world for others. Her dream is to support her community with her stories, as well as creating a company where other artists can come together in celebration of Pelaia and all it has to offer.

Become Part of the Magic & Mystery...

www.patreon.com/RhiDElton

If you want more clues, more magic and more mystery, support me on Patreon.

You'll get exclusive clues, maps, sketches, behind the scenes stories, lore and much more! You'll also be the first to know when a new story is coming out so you can solve the mystery before your friends.

If you join at any tier above $10 you can get mugs, posters, bags and shirts, all with your favourite characters.

www.patreon.com/RhiDElton

Thank you for being part of the magic and supporting an independently published Australian author! Australia's independent authors need the support of their local community to continue to produce the books we all love.

If you enjoyed this book, please leave a positive review online (where you purchased the book or on Goodreads), recommend this book to your friends or family, or purchase another copy to gift to a loved one.

For more stories, become a Patron

www.patreon.com/RhiDElton

BECOME PART OF THE MYSTERY

www.rhiannoneltonauthor.com

 RhiDElton

 RhiannonEltonAuthor

 RhiDElton

 rhiannoneltonauthor

 Rhiannon D. Elton

 RhiDElton

THE WOLFLOCK CASES